SMALL-TOWN FACE-OFF

TYLER ANNE SNELL

This book is for Liz.

Thank you for reading every book, making every birthday cake and understanding I just don't like lemons. Every book I write is because you never stopped supporting me and for that I love you more than you'll ever know. Thank you for being an anchor to a kid who could have been left drifting.

ISBN-13: 978-1-335-72136-5

Small-Town Face-Off

Copyright © 2017 by Tyler Anne Snell

Recycling programs for this product may not exist in your area.

Printed in U.S.A.

www.Harlequin.com

Tyler Anne Snell genuinely loves all genres of the written word. However, she's realized that she loves books filled with sexual tension and mysteries a little more than the rest. Her stories have a good dose of both. Tyler lives in Alabama with her same-named husband and their mini "lions." When she isn't reading or writing, she's playing video games and working on her blog, *Almost There*. To follow her shenanigans, visit tylerannesnell.com.

Books by Tyler Anne Snell

Harlequin Intrigue

The Protectors of Riker County

Small-Town Face-Off

Orion Security

Private Bodyguard
Full Force Fatherhood
Be on the Lookout: Bodyguard
Suspicious Activities

Manhunt

CAST OF CHARACTERS

Sheriff Billy Reed—After a new drug wreaks havoc in the county Billy has spent his entire career trying to protect, he has to team up with a beautiful woman to stop the supplier and save his home. What he doesn't count on is falling in love with her. Or her leaving only to come back two years later with his child in her arms and a madman on her tail.

Mara Copeland—Fighting to get out of the shadow of her criminal father, Mara has tried to win over the residents of Riker County with little success. Plans of staying away from Riker, as well as the sheriff, don't last long after her past comes knocking. Now she's back, this time with a secret daughter in tow.

Alexa—Born a secret to her father, this toddler keeps everyone on their toes as a madman tries to use her against the sheriff.

Bryan Copeland—Father to Mara, this former drug supplier has the sheriff's department and unknown criminal parties racing to find what he's hidden, all while he sits behind prison bars.

Suzy Simmons—Billy's best friend since childhood and his right-hand woman in the field, this chief deputy sheriff will do anything to ensure Alexa's safety.

Cassie Gates—Sheriff department dispatcher who treats Mara with kindness.

Beck—While his motives are unknown at first, he makes it clear that he'll stop at nothing to get to the Copeland family secret.

Prologue

Billy Reed looked down at the body and wished he could punch something. Hard.

"This is ridiculous," Suzy said at his side. "She's not even eighteen."

His partner was right. Courtney Brooks had turned sixteen two weeks ago. The car she had been found in was a birthday present from her father. Billy knew this because he'd known of the girl since she was in middle school. She was a part of one of the many families in the small town of Carpenter, Alabama, who had lived there through at least two generations.

And now she was dead in the back seat of a beat-up Honda.

"Anyone tell her folks yet?" Billy asked. He'd arrived on the scene five minutes after his partner, Suzanne Simmons, had. By the time he'd cut through lunchtime traffic and bumped down the dirt road in his Crown Vic to the spot where poor Courtney had met her end, a set of paramedics, the deputy who had first responded to the call and the boy who had found her were all gathered around, waiting for what was next.

"No, Rockwell wanted to make the call," Suzy answered. Billy raised his eyebrow, questioning why the sheriff would do that when he hadn't even come to the crime scene yet, and she continued. "He's fishing buddies with her dad. He heard Marty call in the name."

Billy could imagine their leader, a man north of sixty with a world of worries to match, breaking the bad news from behind his desk. He'd let his stare get lost in the grain of the oak while he broke a family's heart with news no parents should ever receive.

"There's no signs of foul play, as far as I can tell," Suzy commented. One of the EMTs broke off from the car and headed toward them.

"We both know what this is, Suzy," Billy said. The anger he was nearly getting used to began to flood his system. The deputy could save the EMT time by telling the man he already knew what had killed her. An overdose of a drug called Moxy. The current scourge of Riker County. However, Billy's mother had taught him the importance of being polite. So he listened to the man say that he thought Courtney had been gone a few hours before they'd gotten there, and if the paramedic was a betting man, he'd put his money on an overdose.

"I've already taken pictures, but I'd like to look around again, just in case," Suzy said. Billy was about to follow when a call over the radio drew him to his car instead. He asked dispatch to repeat.

"The sheriff wants you here, Billy," she said. "Now."

That gave him pause but he confirmed he understood. Suzy must have heard, too. She waved him away, saying she could handle it from here. Billy's eye caught the teen who had found Courtney. He was standing with Marty, one of the other deputies from the department, and they were deep in discussion. Every few words he'd glance back at the girl. And each time he looked closer to losing it. He'd likely never seen a dead body before, and judging by his expression, he'd never forget it, either. It made Billy grind his teeth.

No one in Riker County should have that problem. At least, not if Billy had a say about it.

It had been six months since an influx of Moxy hit the county. In that time, Billy had seen four overdoses and an escalation of violence, two of those incidents ending in murder. For all intents and purposes, Moxy brought out the worst tendencies in people and then energized them. While Riker County, its sheriff's department and police departments had had their problems with narcotics in the past, the new drug and its ever-elusive supplier had caught them woefully off guard. It was a fact that kept Billy up at night and one that stayed with him as he drove through the town and then cut his engine in the department's parking lot.

Movement caught his eye, distracting his thoughts, and he realized he was staring at the very man who had called him in. Billy exited the cruiser and leaned against it when the man made no move to go inside the building, arms folded over his chest. Sheriff Rockwell put his cigarette out and stopped in front of him. He looked more world-weary than he had the day before.

"I'm going to cut to the chase, Reed," the sheriff said, leaving no room for greetings. "We need to find the Moxy supplier and we need to find him now. You understand?"

"Yessir," Billy said, nodding.

"Until that happens, I want you to work exclusively on trying to catch the bastard."

"What about Detective Lancaster?" Billy asked. Jamie Lancaster's main focus had been on finding something on the supplier since the second overdose had been reported.

"Lancaster is crap, and we both know it," the sheriff said. "His drive left the second we all had to take a pay cut. No, what we need now is someone whose dedication isn't made by his salary." The sheriff clapped Billy on the shoulder. "In all of my years, I've learned that there's not much that can stand against a person protecting their own. You love not only this town, but the entire county like it's family, Billy."

"I do," Billy confirmed, already feeling his pride swelling.

The sheriff smiled, briefly, and then went stone cold.

"Then go save your family."

Two months later, Billy was sitting in a bar in Carpenter known as the Eagle. In the time since he'd talked to the sheriff in the parking lot, he'd chased every lead known to the department. He'd worked long, hard hours until, finally, he'd found a name.

Bryan Copeland.

A businessman in his upper fifties with thinning gray hair and an affinity for wearing suits despite the Alabama heat, he was running the entire operation from Kipsy. It was the only city within the Riker County Sheriff's Department purview, Carpenter being one of three towns. But where he kept the drugs—whether it was through the city or towns—and when he moved them were mysteries. Which was the reason Billy hadn't had the pleasure of arresting him yet. They couldn't prove anything, not even after two drug dealers admitted who their boss was. Because, according to the judge and Bryan's fancy lawyer, there was no hard evidence. So that was why, late on a Thursday night, Billy Reed was seated at the Eagle finishing off his second beer when a woman sat down next to him and cleared her throat.

"Are you Deputy Reed? Billy Reed?" she asked, voice dropping to a whisper. Billy raised his eyebrow. He didn't recognize the woman. And he would have remembered if he had met her before.

She had long black hair that framed a clear and determined face. Dark eyes that openly searched his expression, trying to figure him out for whatever reason, high cheekbones, pink, pink lips, and an expression that was split between contemplation and caution. All details that created a truly beautiful woman. One who had the deputy's full attention.

"Yes, that's me," he answered. "But I don't think I've had the pleasure."

The woman, who he had placed just under his own age of thirty-two, pasted on a smile and cut her eyes around them before answering.

"I believe you're trying to build a case against my father." Billy immediately went on red alert, ready to field whatever anger or resentment the woman had with him. However, what she said next changed everything. Her dark eyes hardened, resolute. With a voice free of any doubt, she gave Billy exactly what he needed. "And I can help you do just that."

Chapter One

Three years later, Billy Reed was kicking off his shoes, digging into his DVR and turning on a game he'd been meaning to watch for a month. During the season he hadn't had time to keep up with teams or scores but he liked the white noise it produced. And, maybe if it was a close enough game, his focus might leave his work long enough to enjoy it.

He popped off the cap of his beer and smiled at the thought.

He'd been the Riker County sheriff for under two years, although he'd lived his entire life within its lines, just as his father had before him. It was one of the reasons Sheriff Rockwell had personally endorsed Billy to take his place when he'd decided it was time to retire.

"You always want what's best for Riker and I can't think of a better outlook for a sheriff," Rockwell had said. "After what you've helped do for this place already, I can't imagine a better fit."

Billy's eyes traveled to a framed picture of the former sheriff shaking his hand. The picture had been taken during a press conference that had come at one of the most rewarding moments of Billy's career as deputy, when drug supplier ~~Bryan Copeland had been~~ locked behind bars for good.

He didn't know it at the time, but that case would help him become the man he was today—the sheriff who was trying desperately to pretend there was such a thing as a night off. He took a pull on his beer. But as soon as he tried to move his focus to the game on the TV, his phone came to life.

So much for trying.

The caller ID said Suzy. Not a name he'd wanted to see until the next morning. He sighed and answered.

"I just got home, Suzy," he said.

Suzanne Simmons didn't attempt to verbally walk carefully around him. Never mind the fact that he was the boss now. He didn't expect her to, either. She'd been his friend for years.

"That ain't my problem, Sheriff," she snapped. "What *is* my problem is Bernie Lutz's girlfriend drunk and yelling at my desk."

Billy put his beer down on the coffee table, already resigned to the fact that he wouldn't be able to enjoy the rest of it.

"Say again?"

He'd known Suzy since they were in middle school and knew that the short pause she took before answering was her way of trying to rearrange her thoughts without adding in the emotion. As chief deputy she couldn't be seen flying off the handle when her anger flared. The sheriff's right-hand man, or woman in this case, needed to appear more professional than that. Though that hadn't stopped her from expressing herself within the privacy of his office from time to time.

"Bernie Lutz, you remember him?" she asked. "Short guy with that tattoo of his ex-wife on his right arm?"

Billy nodded to himself, mind already going through old files.

"Yeah, drug dealer until he went the straight and narrow about a year ago." Billy remembered something else. "He said he found Jesus and started doing community service when he got out of lockup."

"Well, it looks like he just found a whole lot more than Jesus," Suzy said. "Jessica, his girlfriend, just ran into the station yelling about finding him dead in a ditch when she went out to their house. She's asking for our protection now. And, by asking, I mean yelling for it."

Billy ran his hand down his face, trying to get the facts straight.

"So, did you check out if what she said was true?" he asked.

"Working on it. I tried to get her to come with me to show me exactly where she found him but, Billy, she freaked out big-time. Said they could still be watching her."

Billy stood, already looking for the shoes he'd kicked off when he'd thought his night off might stick. His cowboy hat was always easier to find. He scooped it up off the back of the couch and put it on. The act alone helped focus him even more.

"They?" he asked.

"She claims that two men came to the house last week and asked Bernie for drugs, and when he said he didn't deal anymore, they told him they'd come back and get them both." Suzy lowered her voice a little. "To be honest, I think Jessica is under the influence of *something* right now—why didn't she call us from the scene?—but I sent Dante out there to check it out. I just wanted to give you a heads-up if this thing ends up escalating and poor Bernie really is in a ditch somewhere."

Billy spotted his shoes and went to put them on.

"Go ahead and get descriptions of the men she claims paid them a visit," he said. "They could very well be suspects in a murder. And, if not, at the very least, they could be trying to buy or spread narcotics in the community." His thoughts flew back to Bryan Copeland.

"And we don't want any more of that," she finished.

"No," Billy said. "Definitely not."

"Okay, I'll give you a call when this all pans out."

"Don't worry about it," he said, tying the laces to his shoes. "I'm coming in."

"But—"

"The people of Riker County didn't elect me to sit back when potential murderers could be roaming the streets," he reminded her. "Plus, if there *is* a body and a crime scene, we need to act fast so that the rain doesn't destroy any evidence. Call Matt and tell him to go ahead and head out there. Even if it's a false alarm I'd rather be safe than sorry. Don't let Jessica leave the station until I get there."

Suzy agreed and said goodbye. She might have been his closest friend, but she still knew when to not argue with an order. Even if she had been trying to look out for him.

Billy turned the game off, not bothering to look at the score, and mentally checked out. He tried recalling where Bernie had lived when he'd arrested him and the road that Jessica would travel going there. Billy had grown up in Carpenter, which was one of the three small towns located in Riker County, and Billy had driven all of its roads at least twice. It was the epicenter of a community fused together by humidity, gossip and roots so deep that generations of families never left. Billy Reed was a part of one of those families. He lived in the home he and his father had both grown up in, and a part of him hoped that one day his kids would walk the same hallways. Not that he had any kids. However, it was still a thought that drove him to try and keep the only home he'd ever known a safe, enjoyable one. If Bernie and his past drug habits were back at it, then Billy wanted to nip that in the bud.

Billy tried to rein in thoughts from the past as he searched for his keys, the one item he always seemed to lose, when a knock sounded on the front door. Like a dog trying to figure out a foreign noise, he tilted his head to the side and paused.

It was well past dark and had been raining for the last hour. The list of visitors he'd typically receive was relatively short, considering most wouldn't drop by unannounced. Still, as he walked through the living room to the entryway, he considered the possibility of a friend coming by for a drink or two. Just because he'd become sheriff didn't mean his social life had completely stopped. Then again, for all he knew it could be his mother coming into town early. If so, then he was about to be berated for his lack of Christmas lights and tree despite its being a week away from the holiday. While Billy knew he had to maintain a good image within the community, even when he was off, he hadn't found the time or will to get into a festive mood. Though, if he was being honest with himself, the holidays had lost some charm for him in the last few years. Still, he opened the door with a smile that felt inviting, even genuine.

And immediately was lost for words.

It was like looking in a mirror and recognizing your reflection, yet at the same time still being surprised by it. That's what Billy was going through as he looked at Mara Copeland, dark hair wet from the rain that slid down her poncho, standing on his welcome mat.

"Hey, Billy."

Even her voice pushed Billy deeper into his own personal twilight zone. It kept whatever greeting he had reserved for a normal visitor far behind his tongue.

"I know it's late and I have no business being here but, Billy, I think I need your help."

BILLY DIDN'T MAKE her spell out her situation standing there on his doorstep. He'd regained his composure by the tail end of Mara's plea. Though she could tell it was a struggle.

"Come in," he said, standing back and gesturing wide with his long arms. Mara had almost forgotten how tall he was. Even in the mostly dark space outside his door, she could still make out the appearance of a man who looked the same as he had almost two years before—tall, with broad shoulders and a lean body rather than overly muscled. Lithe, like a soccer player, and no doubt strong, an attractive mix that carried up and through to a hard chin and a prominent nose. His eyes, a wild, ever-moving green, just sweetened the entire pot that was Billy Reed. Mara had realized a long time ago that there wasn't a part of the dark-haired man she didn't find appealing.

Which didn't help what had happened back then.

She hesitated at his invitation to come inside, knowing how meticulous he was with keeping the hardwood in his house clean. Which she clearly was not. The poncho might have kept the clothes underneath dry, but it still was shedding water like a dog would its fur in the summer. Not to mention she hadn't had a hood to keep her long tangles of hair dry.

"Don't worry about it," he said, guessing her thoughts. "It's only water."

His smile, which she'd been afraid she'd broken by her arrival, came back. But only a fraction of it.

The lack of its former affection stung. Then again, what had she expected?

"Sorry to intrude," she said, once they were both shut inside the house. Its warmth eased some of the nerves that had been dancing since she'd gotten into the car that morning, although not nearly enough to keep her stomach from fluttering. Although she'd known her destination since she'd buckled her seat belt, seeing the sheriff in person had stunned her, in a way. Like finding a memory she'd tried to forget suddenly within reach. She started to wonder if he had tried to forget her. "I would have called but I couldn't find your number," she lied.

Billy stood back, giving her space. The small part of his smile that had surfaced was disintegrating. Mara's stomach began to knot. She had a feeling that Billy's politeness was sheer Southern reflex.

And now he was starting to remember exactly who she was.

She didn't blame him or the mistrust that distorted his handsome face next.

Though, that stung a bit, too.

"You could have called the department," he deadpanned. "You might not remember, what with you up and leaving so quickly, but I'm the sheriff. I'm sure if you asked for me they'd patch you right on through."

Mara kept the urge to flinch at bay. In her road trip across Alabama, back to the last place she'd ever thought she'd return—especially with Christmas only days away—a small part of her had hoped Billy would have somehow forgotten or forgiven what she'd done.

That when and if they ever met again, he would smile that dimpled smile that used to make her go weak in the knees and they'd—what?—be friends? Her thoughts had always derailed at that question. They always seemed to when she thought of Billy.

The little girl asleep and hidden beneath the poncho, held up by Mara's arm, didn't help matters.

"I *do* remember that you're the sheriff," she said. "And, you're right, I should have called there, but—" Mara had rehearsed a speech in the car explaining the exact reason she had driven back to Carpenter, back to his house, instead of just calling. Now, however, the words just wouldn't come. All she could find were his eyes, ever searching for an answer. "Well," she started again, trying to find a stronger voice. "It seemed too important to not talk about face-to-face."

Whatever reply Billy had been brewing behind those perfect lips seemed to stall out. His brows pulled together, his nostrils flared and then, just as quickly, his expression began to relax. He took a deep breath.

"Fine," he finally said. "But make it quick. I just got called out."

That was as warm as she'd bet the man was going to be, so she nodded. The simple movement shook water free from the bright yellow poncho covering her. She tried to give him an apologetic look.

"I didn't have an umbrella," she explained.

"You never did," he said, also, she believed, on reflex. Like the nod, it was such a simple statement that Mara wondered if he'd even registered he'd said it at all. "Here, let me help with that." Billy reached out and took the bag from her shoulder. Any mother might recognize it as a diaper bag, though it was designed to look like an oversized purse, but she could tell Billy Reed hadn't caught on to it yet.

Or the bulge beneath the poncho.

She must have really thrown him for a loop.

"Thanks. Do you have a bag or something I could put this poncho in?" She motioned to the very thing keeping their conversation from diving headlong into the foreign topic of kids.

"Yeah, give me a sec." He set her bag on the entryway bench and headed toward the kitchen. It gave Mara a moment to take two deep breaths before letting each out with a good shake.

It had been two years since she'd seen Billy Reed. More than that since she'd met him in a bar, ready to do her best to help him take down the only family she'd had left. Now here she was, standing in his house, dripping on the hardwood.

"This is all I have to put it in," he said, coming back. His smile was still gone but at least he wasn't stone-faced.

"Oh, thanks," Mara said to the Walmart bag he extended. She didn't take it. "Actually, I'm going to need your help with this one. I don't want to drop her."

And, just like that, Billy Reed must have finally looked at her—*really* looked at her—taking in the large bulge beneath the poncho. Wordlessly, he helped her pull it off. He stood there, eyes wide, as the dark-haired little girl came into view. She wiggled at the sudden light but, thankfully, stayed asleep. One little blessing that Mara would more than take.

"This is Alexa," Mara introduced her. She watched as his eyes widened. They swept over the little girl with attention she knew he was proud of. For a moment she forgot why she'd come. So many times over the last two years she'd thought about this meeting. Would it happen? What would he say? What would *she* say? However, Mara reminded herself that she hadn't come back to Carpenter because she'd decided to. No, a man and his threats had made that decision for her. Mara cleared her throat. It was now or never. "Billy, meet your daughter."

Chapter Two

Billy, bless him, didn't say a thing for a good minute. Though his eyes ran the gamut of emotions.

Mara took a tentative step toward him, arm still holding their daughter up, and opened her mouth to speak, but Billy's phone went off in his pocket, ringing too loudly to ignore.

He shook off the spell he'd fallen into, though when he spoke, his voice wasn't as strong as it had been before.

"Please, hold that thought. I have to take this," he said, pulling his phone out. He didn't look at the caller ID as he answered. "Reed."

Mara's mouth closed as a woman's voice filled the space between them. She didn't stop for breath as she relayed whatever she needed to the man. Slowly his attention split and refocused on the new information. His brow furrowed and his eyes took on a look Mara knew all too well.

This was Work Billy and she'd come at a bad time. That much was clear.

"Okay, thanks," he said when the woman had finished. "I'll be there in twenty."

Mara's stomach fell as Billy ended the call. She didn't know what she had expected of the man she'd left with no more than a note on his pillow and no hint whatsoever that she was pregnant with his child. But his taking a work call hadn't been on the list of possibilities. She straightened her back. Alexa squeezed her little arms around Mara's neck in her sleep. The slight movement wasn't missed by Billy. He looked at his daughter before his eyes cut back to her.

"You have a world of explaining to do," he started, voice low. He had finally landed on an emotion. Anger. "First you just up and leave, then you don't talk to me for two years, and now you're saying that—" He stopped his voice from going any louder. Without breaking eye contact he reached for the raincoat on the wall next to them. "A body has just been found and I need to try and get to the crime scene before this rain messes everything up. If it hasn't already." He slid into the coat. "I'm sorry." He ran his finger across the brim of his hat. "It's been a long day and I didn't expect to see you." His eyes trailed down to Alexa before meeting Mara's again. His expression softened, if only a little. "I would ask you along, but I don't think a crime scene in the rain is a good place to have this talk."

"I'll agree to that," Mara said. Before she could add anything the sheriff's expression changed again. It became alert, ready.

"Wait, you said you needed my help?" he asked.

The angles of his face seemed to go tight. While Mara had no doubt he was ready to listen to her with all of his attention, he was also still thinking about the crime scene. The sound of pounding rain probably wasn't helping.

"I can wait until you're done," she said. The urgency that had driven her from their home that morning had ebbed considerably, especially now that she was there, standing in Billy's house. Maybe she had been foolish to leave so suddenly and come running back to Carpenter.

And its sheriff.

"Are you sure?" She could see his resolve splitting. She nodded.

"I can go check in to the hotel off Miller Street, if you think it will be a bit."

"Why don't you just wait here? It's not like you don't know your way around." Heat rushed up to Mara's cheeks at the comment. She doubted he'd meant to stir up old memories. He was just stating a fact. She *did* know her way around, having spent countless hours there trying to plan a way to stop her father. A pursuit that had had unexpected outcomes.

"Oh, I wouldn't want to intr—"

"Mara." Billy's voice took on a low edge. "Stay."

An easy command for any smart woman to follow from Billy Reed.

Alexa stirred in her arms.

"Okay," she relented. It would be nice not to have to run Alexa back out into the bad weather. Plus, she doubted after the information she'd just hit him with, Billy would leave his house until he had the whole story. She couldn't blame him. "I'll wait until you get back."

An expression she didn't quite understand flashed across Billy's face, but when he spoke his voice was normal, considering everything.

"Help yourself to any food in the fridge," he said. "I'll be back as soon as I can."

Mara thanked him and moved out of his way as he went out into the storm. The Billy she'd known years before hadn't changed. Justice and protecting those within his jurisdiction still prevailed.

"Well, Alexa," Mara said once she'd heard his Tahoe leave. "This is the Reed family home."

A little uncertainly, Mara slipped off her shoes and padded through the entryway and into the living room. Surprisingly, or maybe not, nothing seemed to have changed since the last time she'd been in the house. The old dark hardwood grounded a room that had been the heart of the Reed family for two generations. Sure, some of the furniture had changed—the black leather couch certainly hadn't been Billy's mother's choice, and neither had the plasma flat-screen—but the cozy feel of a house well loved and well lived-in hadn't diminished one bit.

Mara kept on her tour with a growing smile. From the living room she went to the kitchen, the dining room and the open office. She was looking for clues that might tell her what had happened to Billy since she'd left Carpenter. The family pictures of the Reeds still dotted the walls, including some new additions and marriages, while other pictures specific only to Billy also popped up occasionally. Mara stopped and smiled at one in particular that caught her eye.

Standing in front of a crowd of Riker County residents was the dark-haired man, moments after he'd been officially elected sheriff.

The old affection began to break through an emotional dam she'd spent years building. Then, just as quickly, she was back to that morning, when she'd stood on her front porch across from the stranger who had threatened her life and the life of her child. If anyone could deal with the mystery man it was the Riker County sheriff.

Alexa moved in her arms. This time she woke up.

The cold that had started to spread in the pit of Mara's stomach turned to warmth.

"Well, hello there," she whispered.

Alexa looked up at her mom. Just shy of fifteen months, the toddler might not have known much about the world, but that had never stopped her beautiful green eyes from being curious.

Just like her father's.

IT TOOK FIFTEEN minutes to get to the ditch that held Bernie Lutz's body. Billy could have taken three hours—hell, three days—and still not have been able to completely process what had just happened. A herd of elephants could have stampeded alongside his Tahoe as he navigated the muddy back road and it wouldn't have distracted him. Mara's sudden reappearance alone would have stunned him. But this? Alexa? Mara Copeland on his doorstep with a baby?

His baby.

"Get a hold of yourself, Billy," he said out loud. "You've got a job to do first."

Had Mara been wearing a wedding ring? Billy shook his head. He needed to focus on one thing at a time. He needed to put everything that wasn't Bernie Lutz out of his mind. At least for the moment.

He sighed.

Yet, there Mara had been. Staring up at him through her long dark lashes, asking for help.

And he'd just left.

His phone went off, dancing on the dash before he answered. This time it was Matt Walker, currently Riker County's only detective, thanks to the retirement of his former partner. Like Suzy, Matt was direct when he spoke about work.

"Henry got a tarp up, Billy," he yelled over the weather. "But the road runoff is washing everything away. I went ahead and called in the county coroner."

Billy swore.

"It hasn't rained in weeks, and the one time we need it dry is the one time all hell breaks loose."

"It could be worse," Matt said. "We could be the body in the ditch."

Billy nodded.

"You're right," he said, sobering. "I'm a few minutes out. If the coroner gets there before me, go ahead and load him up. Maybe if we act fast enough we can salvage some evidence."

"Ten-four." Billy started to hang up but Matt cut back in. "And Billy? Just from looking at him, I'm going to say that his girlfriend might have been telling some kind of truth. He's beaten pretty badly. His death wasn't fast, by any means. See you when you get here."

He ended the call.

Thoughts of the past half hour were replaced by the need to solve a murder.

IT WAS JUST before midnight when Billy unlocked his front door. The storm raged on. Every part of him was soaking wet, and his boots and jeans were more mud than anything. He didn't even try to keep the floor clean. Instead, he sloshed inside and stripped in the entryway.

It wasn't until he was starting to pull off his shirt that he spotted the bright yellow poncho sticking out of a Walmart bag. He froze as his brain detached from work life and zipped right back to his personal one.

Mara.

With more attention to the noise he was making, he left his shirt on and, instead, got out of his boots. Only one light was on. He followed it into the living room. For one moment he thought it was empty—that Mara had left again, this time with his daughter in tow—but then he spotted a mass of dark hair cascading over the arm of the couch. Coming around to face it, he was met with a sight that used to be familiar.

Mara was asleep, body pulled up so that her knees were close to her stomach, making her look impossibly small. It wasn't the first time he'd come home after work to find her in that exact spot, lights still on, waiting for him. Even when he'd tell her not to wait up, Billy would come in after a long day to find her there. She'd never once complained. Seeing her lying there, face soft and unguarded, Billy took a small moment for himself to remember what it felt like to come home to her. But it didn't last.

There had been too many nights between then and now. Ones where he'd come home to an empty house, wondering why she'd gone.

I'm sorry, but it's over.

Billy shook his head at the one sentence that had changed everything between them and looked at the one idea he'd never entertained after Mara had gone.

Alexa was tucked within her mother's arms, simultaneously fitting and not fitting in the space between. Her hair was dark, but still lighter than his, and it fell just past her shoulders and, from the looks of it, was as thick as her mother's. Before he could police his thoughts, a smile pulled up the corners of his lips.

He might not have known her the day before, but that didn't stop the affection for the little girl.

And, just like before, the feeling of warmth, however brief, was gone.

Why had she been kept a secret?

Billy took a step back. While he had questions, he didn't want to wake either one, but the creak in the floor that had been there since his father was a child sounded under his weight. Mara's eyes fluttered opened and immediately found him.

"I tried to be quiet," he whispered.

Mara shook her head and slowly sat up while trying to disengage herself from the toddler.

"No, I'm sorry," she whispered back once she managed to get free. "I didn't mean to fall asleep."

She followed him through the entryway and into the dining room, far enough away that they could talk in normal tones.

And, boy, did they have a lot to talk about.

"What time is it?" she asked, taking a seat at the table. She stifled a yawn.

"Close to midnight. I was gone a lot longer than I thought I would be," he admitted. Billy took a seat opposite her. "This storm couldn't have come at a worse time."

Mara nodded, but the movement was sluggish. He was tired, too. It was time to stop delaying and finally ask the current question on his mind.

"Mara, why are you here?"

Chapter Three

"A man came to my house this morning and asked about my father," Mara said, knowing full well that once the words were out there Billy wouldn't forget them. Finding a way to take down her father—to catch him in the act—had been an emotional and physical drain on them both. The collective hope that Billy would save Riker County had pressed down heavily on him, while betraying the only family she'd had had never left Mara's mind.

As if an invisible hand had found the strings to his puppet, Billy's entire body snapped to attention.

"They wanted Bryan?"

But he's in prison, Mara silently finished.

"The man didn't want *him*," she said out loud instead. "The guy wanted something important of my father's and I needed to tell him where it was. I had no idea what he was talking about."

Billy's dark brow rose in question. "Something important," he deadpanned.

"He didn't say what, past that," she admitted, recalling how the man had been careful when choosing his words. "But what really spooked me was when he said he wanted to take over what my father had built, my family's business. And I don't think he was talking about my dad's old accounting job."

Billy's forehead creased in thought. She could almost see the red flags popping up behind his eyes.

"Moxy," he supplied.

She nodded. "I told him I had no part in that slice of my father's life, but he didn't seem to care," she continued. She twisted her hands together, and when she recounted what happened next her stomach was a knot of coldness. "Then he saw Alexa playing in the house behind me. He told me that I might change my mind if I had the right incentive."

Billy's body managed to take on an even greater tension.

"What did he want you to change your mind about?" he asked. "Telling him the location of *something important* or wanting nothing to do with your father's past business?"

Mara sighed.

"I don't know. After he looked Alexa's way, I told him he needed to leave." Mara let her gaze drop. "He didn't argue, but he did say he'd be seeing me again soon."

Billy's chair scraped the hardwood as he pushed back. Mara could feel her eyes widen in surprise as she readjusted her attention to his expression.

Anger. And it definitely wasn't meant for her this time.

"I'm assuming he didn't give you a name," Billy

said, walking out of the dining room and disappearing. He was back a second later with a small notepad and a pen in his hands.

"Just a first name. Beck."

"And did you call the cops?"

A burst of heat spread up her neck and pooled in her cheeks. Mara had *thought* about filing a police report, but the mention of her father had thrown her completely off-kilter. What she would *normally* have done went out the window. Instead, her thoughts had flown south to Riker County. And the only man who had ever made her feel safe. Suddenly, that feeling that had burned so strongly hours before when she'd packed the car and taken Alexa on a trip across Alabama seemed rash.

"No," she admitted. "I should have but—well, I thought if someone was trying to start up my father's business again that they would start it here. I thought that I should—I don't know—warn you or something." Again, her words sounded lame compared to what she wanted to say. But at least they were true. In his prime, Bryan Copeland had grown a drug network that nearly swallowed the whole of Riker County. His dealings had cost the lives of several residents, including teenagers. Not to mention a cascade of repercussions that were harder to measure. The fact that all of her father's former connections hadn't been found was one that had always made the man in front of her nervous. Part of her father's business hadn't been accounted for…which meant that if this Beck person *was* trying to start up again, it would only stand to reason he might have found the people law enforcement hadn't. Or maybe that's what Beck was looking for.

For the first time since he'd stepped back through the door, Billy's expression softened a fraction. The lines of tension in his shoulders, however, did not.

"Could you describe to me what this Beck guy looks like?" He flipped open the notebook and clicked his pen. "And did you see his car?"

"Yes and yes."

Mara spent the next few minutes painting a picture of the stranger named Beck until Billy was satisfied it was enough to try and look him up through the department's database.

Mara thought it curious that Billy never asked where she was currently living. It made her wonder if he'd looked her up at all in the last two years. She hadn't gone far, but far enough that Riker County had been firmly in her rearview.

"I want you to come to the station with me tomorrow," Billy said, closing the notepad. "I'm going to see if the sketch artist from the state agency can come in and work with you. Maybe the new guy can draw us a good picture to work with if this Beck person isn't on our list of people with warrants out on them."

"So, you think Beck was serious?"

Mara sat straighter. The possibility of someone revitalizing Moxy, or any drug, within the community using the foundation her father had laid was finally sinking in. Just another reason for the residents of Riker County to despise her and her family. "You think he's really going to try and start up where Dad left off?"

Billy let out a long breath. He ran his hands through his hair. How attractive she still found him was not lost on Mara. Looking at him now, a well-built, fine-tuned man with miles and miles of good-will and good intentions, she could feel the stirring of feelings she needed to stay still. Not to mention the heat of attraction that always lit within her when Billy was anywhere near. But now wasn't the time or place. If there was a chance he could forgive her for leaving, she doubted he'd forgive her for keeping their daughter a secret—a topic of conversation she was sure would take place once the cop side of him was done flexing his professional muscles.

The sheriff cleared his throat. His eyes hardened. He had something to say and she doubted she'd like it.

"We found Bernie Lutz in a ditch tonight," he started. Mara felt recognition flare but couldn't keep it burning long enough to connect. Billy helped her out. "He was one of the drug dealers your dad used who escaped the serious charges after Bryan went to court." There it was.

"The one with the ex-wife tattoo," she said. He nodded.

"This was never confirmed, but the story his girl-friend spun was that two men came to their house looking for something the other day. Whatever it was, Bernie didn't know or didn't tell. This could all be a coincidence, but you know me, I don't believe in those." Billy put his finger on the paper he'd just written on. He jabbed it once. "Not only do I think this mystery man is going to try to start up your dad's old business, but I think he might have already started."

BILLY WAITED FOR Mara to process everything and then excused himself to go to his room. He slipped into his attached bathroom and splashed cold water on his face. The night had thrown him several curve-balls and he hadn't hit one of them.

Even if he filtered out Mara's sudden reappear-ance and the absolute bombshell that was their daugh-ter, Billy still had Bryan Copeland's legacy to worry about. Whoever this Beck person was, Billy would be damned if he was going to let him repeat what had caused Riker County so much pain years ago. Espe-cially not during the holiday. That was no present any family should have to get.

Billy splashed another wave of water on his face. He stayed hunched over, resting his elbows on the edge of the sink, and kept his eyes closed. There. He could feel the weight of Riker County's newest burden settling against him. It pressed down on his shoulders and kept going until it hit his chest. No, he wasn't going to stand by while the residents of his county endured another Bryan Copeland incident.

Billy opened his eyes.

Not while he was sheriff.

He dried his face, and without changing out of his wet clothes, he walked out to find Mara, his mind al-ready made up.

She was standing in the living room, Alexa asleep

in her arms. Her bag was thrown over her shoulder and her expression was already telling him goodbye.

"You're leaving."

Mara's cheeks reddened but her answer came out clear, concrete.

"Yes, but not town. To be honest, I don't like Beck knowing where I live so I don't want to go back there just yet," she answered. "Plus, to be even more honest, I'm really tired. The faster we get to the hotel, the happier I'll be."

Billy wasn't a complicated man. At least, he didn't think he was. Yet, standing there a few feet from a woman who had left him in the dust, he knew he shouldn't have felt any joy at her admission that she was staying. Or an ounce of desire from looking at her hardened nipples through her light pink T-shirt—the result, he guessed, from the AC he had turned up despite the cool they were getting from the storm—or how her jeans hugged her legs just right. But he did.

"Stay here instead," Billy said before he realized he'd even thought it. Mara's eyes widened a fraction. Her cheeks darkened slightly. "The guest bedroom is free, the sheets are clean and you don't have to drive in the rain to get there. Plus, Miller's parking lot looked pretty full. Probably lousy with in-laws and extended family members that no one wants in their house."

He grinned, trying to drive his point home. It didn't work.

"I don't think it's a good idea," Mara said, eyes straying from his. He wondered if she knew he was thinking about her naked and against him. It was a fleeting thought, but by God it was there. "I've already upset your life enough by coming here."

Billy cleared his throat and tried to clear the feelings of attraction he was currently wading through. He needed some space from her, but he wasn't about to let her leave without a fight, either. Something he wished he could have done two years before.

"Then stay in the guesthouse," he offered.

Mara met his gaze.

"I finished it last summer," he explained, remembering she hadn't known he'd thrown all of his spare time into finishing the apartment that used to be the detached garage. It had been less for his mother when she came for long visits and more of a distraction. "Come on, Mara," he continued when she still seemed to be weighing her options. He moved closer but stopped when the floorboard squeaked. It earned a small movement from Alexa. Billy let himself look at the little girl before fixing her mama with a look he hoped didn't show how hard it was to just talk to her. "Please, Mara. Just stay."

Mara shifted Alexa so she was more firmly on her hip. A wisp of a smile pulled up her lips but it blew away before she answered.

"Okay, we'll stay in the guesthouse if it really doesn't bother you."

Billy nodded and moved to grab her bag. His eyes lingered on Alexa but he didn't ask to hold her. He couldn't be a father right now. Not when things in Riker County were starting to heat up. Not when

Mara had attracted the attention of a mysterious man who had no problem threatening children. Not when he'd been in contact with Mara for less than an hour and was already having trouble focusing on anything else. He shouldered the bag and led the two down the hall and to the back door, grabbing an umbrella in the process.

It wasn't raining as hard as it had been, but it was enough to warrant pulling Mara close to him to stay dry beneath the umbrella. She didn't move away or argue as she folded into his left arm and against his side. The inner war he was fighting was downright impossible to ignore as they walked in silence along the stone path that led to the guesthouse door. Billy pulled the keys out of his pocket and unlocked it.

"Here you go," he said, voice low, even to his ears.

He watched as she stepped inside and wordlessly looked around the living space. A kitchenette, three-piece bathroom and a small bedroom made up the rest of the apartment. He'd built on to expand it but everything was still small. At least it was private.

And far enough away from him that he'd never know if she left.

"Oh, it's beautiful, Billy," Mara said after a moment. "You did a wonderful job."

Billy would have taken the compliment with pride if anyone else had given it at any other time. But Mara's words flipped a switch within him. He felt his body stiffen, his expression harden. The pain of finding her note on his pillow came back to him in full.

"I'll come get you at seven," he said. He stepped

back out into the rain but didn't look away from those dark eyes that made him crazy. "And, Mara, try not to leave this time. Once we get this guy you're going to tell me exactly why you kept my daughter a secret."

Chapter Four

Mara and Alexa were up and ready when Billy knocked on the guesthouse door the next morning.

"You're late," Mara greeted him, a hand on her hip. She nodded to the clock on the wall behind her. It was ten past seven.

"I thought I'd give you some wiggle room," he admitted. He looked down at Alexa, who was, for the first time, wide-awake since they'd shown up on his doorstep. Her attention stayed on the stuffed dog in her hands as she played on the floor.

"There's no such thing as wiggle room when you have a toddler," she said with a smirk. It was meant as a quick comment, but Billy couldn't help but wonder about the foundation it was born from. When had Mara learned that lesson? Whenever it was, all he knew was it was without him.

Mara's smirk sank into a frown. She cleared her throat, humor gone.

"Listen, about Alexa," she started, but Billy was already a step ahead of her. He held his hand up for her to stop.

"Again, I want to have this talk. I really would like to know why you kept my daughter from me," he said, serious. "But not right now." Mara opened and closed her mouth, like a fish out of water, trying to find what words, Billy didn't know, but he didn't have time to find out. "Right now we need to find Beck and figure out what it is he's done and is trying to do so we can stop him," he continued. "My first priority is to keep you two safe. You can tell me all about your reasoning for not letting me know I was a father later." While he spoke with what he was trying to pass off as authority, he couldn't help but hear the anger at the end of it.

He'd spent most of the night lying awake in bed, coming up with a plan of action for the day. In the plan was a large section related to how he wanted to handle Mara and Alexa. After hours of no sleep, he'd decided the best way to do his job—to keep everyone safe—was to detach himself emotionally from the dark-haired beauties in front of him.

However, maybe that was going to be harder than he'd thought.

"Okay," Mara finally said. "I'll follow you to the station."

She grabbed her bag and scooped up Alexa. The little girl clung to her stuffed animal with laser-like focus. Billy wondered what other toys she liked.

"There's a coffeehouse that opened up across the street that has pretty good breakfast," Billy said as he locked up the guesthouse behind them.

"I actually packed enough cereal to last for weeks

for this one," Mara said, motioning to Alexa. "She's a nut about Cheerios as soon as she wakes up in the morning." Alexa swung her head up to face Mara and let out a trill of laughter. It surprised Billy how he instantly loved the sound. "Yeah, you've already scarfed down two helpings, haven't you, you little chowhound?" Mara cooed at the girl. Together they laughed, bonded in their own little world.

One that Billy didn't know.

He cleared his throat and Mara straightened.

"But," she continued, expression turning to the same focus her daughter had worn before. "If they have good coffee, I won't turn that down." She smiled but it didn't last long. "And, Billy, I know it's not my place, but I noticed you didn't have a tree or any Christmas decorations or lights…"

Billy sighed.

No matter what was happening in their lives, leave it to the women of the South to still care about Christmas decorations.

THE RIKER COUNTY Sheriff's Department was located in the very heart of Carpenter but was by no means in an extravagant headquarters. That never stopped Billy from feeling a boost of pride when it swung into view. Placed between the county courthouse and the local television station, the sheriff's department was two stories tall and full of men and women tasked with protecting their Southern home.

Wrapped in faded orange brick and concrete, its entrance opened up to a street almost every Carpenter resident had to drive along to get somewhere, while its parking lot around back butted up against a business park that housed a bistro, a coffeehouse and a clothing boutique called Pepper's. Billy and Mara angled their cars into the assigned and guest parking, respectively, and headed straight to the coffeehouse. Billy had tried to convince Mara to ride with him but she'd pointed out his day could get hectic and she liked having the option of her own transportation. Not to mention the car seat was already in her car. Billy decided not to push the topic since she was a flight risk. Instead, he decided to act like everything was normal when they went into the coffeehouse. There they earned a double take from one half of the owner pair known as the Chambers. Becky, a bigger woman with short hair and an even shorter temper, was surprisingly tactful as she addressed them.

"Well, Sheriff, can't say I was expecting to see you on your day off," she started, then she switched her attention to Mara and Alexa. "And certainly not with two lovely ladies in tow."

Billy ignored the affectionate part of the statement, along with what felt suspiciously like pride, and showed just how happy he was about being in on his off day with a frown.

"A sheriff's job is never done," he said solemnly.

"Not with that attitude." Becky winked at Mara, but the dark-haired beauty's gaze had been drawn to the corner booth.

"I'll take my usual," Billy said. "She'll take one of

your mocha iced coffee concoctions I always complain about."

Becky raised her eyebrow.

"Does the lady not get a say?" she asked, voice beginning to thread with disapproval. Her changing tone must have snagged Mara's attention. She turned back to them with a small smile.

"She definitely does, but this one here apparently hasn't forgotten my guilty mocha pleasures," she said. "With whipped cream, too, if you have it, please."

Becky seemed appeased that Billy wasn't rolling over Mara and went about making their drinks while they hung off to the side of the counter. Billy expected Mara to comment about his remembering her favorite caffeinated drink but the woman seemed focused on the corner booth again. So much so that she hardly noticed when he moved close enough to drop his voice so no one else heard him.

"What's going on?"

Alexa looked up from her place on Mara's hip and stared at Billy with an expression caught somewhere between inquisitive and concerned. He couldn't help but stare right back into those green eyes. Like looking into a mirror when it came to the same green.

"That's Donna Ramsey," Mara answered, in an equally low voice. Billy broke his staring contest with Alexa and angled his body to glance at the other side of the room. True to her words, Donna Ramsey was sitting in the corner booth, head bent over the magazine and coffee on the table in front of her. He nodded.

"It is."

Billy watched as Mara's face grew tight. She furrowed her brow.

"Do you know Donna personally?" he asked, his own concern pushing to the forefront. Mara shook her head.

"I've only spoken to her once."

"About?"

He knew Mara well enough to know that her thoughts had turned dark. From anger or sadness or something else, though, he couldn't tell.

"About my father," she answered, voice nearly lost amidst the clatter of the espresso machine. Mara lost her dark look and replaced it with something akin to nonchalance.

"Don't worry," she said. "It was before I left and nothing I didn't already know."

Becky bustled into view before he could question Mara further. She handed them their drinks and looked at Billy.

"Remember, Sheriff, complaining always makes problems ten times worse," she said sagely. "So stop complaining and start drinking some of the best coffee this town has to offer."

Billy couldn't help but smirk.

"You got it, Becky."

Mara waved goodbye while Alexa giggled, and soon the three of them were walking to the back of the station.

"I like her," Mara commented.

"Next time you order from her, tell her that," Billy said. "Suzy did and now she gets a discount."

Mara laughed and Alexa started to babble. Billy craned his neck to look down at her face. Whatever she was saying must have been normal because Mara didn't skip a beat.

"Suzy," she started. "I—I haven't seen her since you were sworn in."

They had made it to the back door used by employees only. Billy pulled out his key and went ahead and addressed the elephant in their shared room.

"She's still one of the few in the department who knows about us working together to bring down your dad. I never told anyone else about the other us. Or what we used to be," he amended. With his key hanging in the lock he looked over his shoulder to the woman he'd been ready to spend forever with and then to their child. "I'll leave it up to you what personal details you want to disclose to my staff. And I'll follow your lead. But whatever you choose to do today, don't think I won't undermine it tomorrow if I need to."

Then Billy opened the door and headed inside, mind already going into work mode. He had a murder to solve and a man named Beck to find.

IT WAS COMFORTING, in a way, to walk into the department alongside Billy. Because, unlike their lives in the last two years, the building hadn't changed. At least, not any way that Mara could tell.

They took the back hallway that ran behind dispatch and the break room and turned the corner to where Mara knew offices lined one of the hallways that led back toward the lobby. Billy's office was smack dab in the middle of the others. His nameplate shone with importance. Mara couldn't help but feel some pride creep in at the sight of it.

"Walden, the sketch artist, said he'd be here by eight thirty," Billy said, walking them past his office. "Until then I'd like you to officially make a statement about this Beck fellow. I'm going to double-check that no one fitting Beck's description is a part of an open case with us or local PD." He stopped two doors over and motioned her inside. It was the conference room and it definitely wasn't empty.

Mara felt her cheeks immediately heat at the sight of mostly familiar faces. Alexa tucked her head into the side of her neck, suddenly shy. Mara didn't blame her. Billy motioned to an open chair, one of many, around the long table in the middle of the room. Mara sat down with tired grace. Alexa's sudden shyness didn't help either one of them adjust from standing to sitting down.

"Most of you already know Mara, and Mara you know them." Billy continued to stand. He motioned to Suzy, Matt Walker and Dane Jones. The last time she'd seen them Suzy had been a deputy along with Billy, Matt had been a deputy, too and Dane had been on his way to being sheriff. Now, sitting across from them, Mara doubted their titles were the same. She wondered what title Dane had now but she wasn't about to ask for clarification.

On the same side of the table was the one face she didn't recognize, a pretty young woman with curly blond hair and a smile that looked genuine. Before Mara could stop the thought, she wondered if Billy found the woman pretty, too.

"Mara, this is Cassie Gates," Billy said, making the introduction. "She's training to be a dispatcher." Mara couldn't stop the confusion that must have crossed her expression as to why a dispatcher, a *trainee* dispatcher, was in the room with them when the woman answered the question herself.

"I'm the youngest of six siblings, most of whom have a kid or two under their belt, so I'm very experienced in the art of keeping little ones entertained when their mamas need to do something important," she said, voice as sweet as her appearance. She flashed a quick smile at Alexa and addressed the toddler directly. "And what's your name? I bet it's something pretty."

The entire room seemed to wait as Alexa peeked out at Cassie. There was nothing like waiting for a toddler's judgment. Seemingly based on some unknown factor, there was no telling how a child would react to something new. That included people. However, instead of hiding away again, Alexa seemed intrigued. She looked back at Mara for a moment, as if asking for permission.

"This is Alexa," Mara introduced them with a smile, showing Alexa her approval of the woman next to them. She might have been a stranger to her but she wasn't to Billy. Mara trusted his judgment. And Alexa trusted Mara's.

"Well, what do you know. That *is* a pretty name,"

Cassie said, animation in her words. It reeled in Alexa's attention. The blonde reached for a bag next to her. From her seat Mara could see it was filled with books and toys. Billy had prepared for the morning, despite short notice. "If it's okay with your mama, how about we go next door and play in the sheriff's office? You could even help me read this." Cassie held up the children's book *Pat the Pet* and Alexa nearly lost it.

"Dog! Dog," she exclaimed, already trying to get off Mara's lap.

It earned a surprised laugh from Cassie. Mara reached into her own bag and produced the same book.

"Welcome to her favorite book," she said to the trainee. "She likes petting the dog the most."

Mara gave Cassie permission to go next door and play, since Alexa seemed to have lost any doubt about the woman as soon as the book had come into view. Mara didn't miss the way Billy's eyes stuck to the cover of the copy Mara had brought along. With more than a twinge of guilt, she realized that, like the stranger who was Cassie, he hadn't had a clue in the world what his daughter did and didn't like.

But Mara couldn't change what she'd already done and turned to face what was left of the group. The men each gave her a friendly smile. Suzy, on the other hand, gave her a stiff nod. While the other two had known about their working relationship, Suzy alone had known about Mara and Billy's romantic one and her sudden departure. As one of Billy's closest friends, Suzy probably knew better than even her how he'd handled it, too.

"Now, Mara," Billy started, setting a tape recorder in the middle of the table. "If you could start at the beginning, when the man named Beck visited you."

Mara repeated the story she'd told Billy the night before, making sure to give them as clear a picture as she could of Beck. Before she could finish describing his clothes and car, however, a man knocked at the door. Despite his dark complexion, Mara mentally likened his expression to "looks like he's seen a ghost."

"Excuse me, Sheriff, we have a problem," he interrupted. Like fans passing on a wave in a football stadium's stands, Billy and his staff became visibly tense.

"What is it?" The man hesitated and looked at Mara. "It's fine. Tell me," Billy added, showing that Mara's presence didn't bother them with whatever news he had.

Which wasn't good news at all.

"We just got a call about two teens who are being taken to the hospital," he started. "They were both overdoses."

Mara's eyes widened. She asked him what everyone else was thinking.

"Of what?"

Bless him, he didn't hesitate in responding to her, though Mara would have been happier if it had been with a different answer.

"Moxy. They overdosed on Moxy."

Chapter Five

Billy tried to not feel like he was suddenly several years in the past, staring at the deceased Courtney Brooks in her car. But there he was, sitting in a conference room and feeling exactly as he had then.

Sad.

Guilty.

Angry.

If he had been alone, he would probably have thrown something. Instead, the best he could do was toss a few expletives in the direction of Deputy Dante Mills, who, thankfully, didn't seem to take open frustration personally.

"They were at the abandoned drive-in theater out past the town limits," Deputy Mills continued. "The owner of the gas station across the street saw their cars hadn't moved in a while and decided to investigate with her husband. Neither had ID on them. As far as their status, it was unclear how bad the damage was, other than they needed medical attention ASAP."

Billy had heard enough. He turned to Suzy, who rose at the same time.

"We're going to the hospital," he told her. Then to Matt, "And I want you to go to the theater grounds and look around. Talk to the gas station owner, too." Billy turned to Dane Jones and a look of understanding passed between them. For his own personal reasons, Dane had taken himself out of the running for sheriff and, instead, applied for Captain of Investigative Bureau within the department after Rockwell had retired. He preferred fighting the good fight from behind a desk instead of out on the streets. Billy couldn't blame him after what had happened to the man years before. Some cases just went south and there wasn't anything anyone could do about it. That was a lesson Dane hadn't let himself learn yet.

"I'll finish up here and see what we can do to find this Beck person. See if we can't connect some dots to Bernie Lutz, too," Dane said. "I'll even give Chief Hawser a call and see if he's had anything come across his desk."

Billy nodded. It was a good idea to go ahead and touch base with Carpenter's police department. Although Billy was sheriff of Riker County, the town of Carpenter and the city of Kipsy had their own police departments and anything that happened within those municipalities was their jurisdiction. Bernie's body and the overdoses had been found just outside the town limits, which meant Billy was running the show. But he didn't have an ego too big to not have an open dialogue with the local PD. He happened to be a fan of Chief Hawser, too.

Billy finally looked at Mara. Her expression was

pinched and worn at the same time. He assumed the news had put her on the line between the present and the past, just as it had him, anger and guilt both squarely on her shoulders. He wanted to go to her, even took a small step forward, but caught himself.

"The sketch artist should be here soon," Billy said. "You can wait in my office if he takes too long."

Mara's jaw tightened.

"As long as you figure out who's doing this," she said.

"Believe me. I will."

Suzy wordlessly followed him to the parking lot and into his Tahoe as the rest of the department went on with their tasks. She kept quiet as he pulled away from the department and got on the main road that would lead them to Carpenter's hospital. However, no sooner had they passed the first intersection when Suzy asked the one question Billy knew she would.

"Is Alexa yours?"

Billy had already resigned himself to following whatever lead Mara wanted to take about telling the department who the father was. But she hadn't expressed herself one way or the other.

"Yes," he answered, surprising himself. "I just found out last night."

He cast a look over at his friend. Suzy, a mother herself, didn't seem to pass any judgment either way on the information. Instead, she kept her gaze focused out the windshield.

"She's a cute kid," she said, as if they were talking about the weather. "I'm glad she didn't get your nose."

Billy laughed. He somehow felt better.

THE SKETCH ARTIST'S name was Walden and he very much looked like what Mara suspected a Walden would look like. Slightly rounded in the gut, thick glasses, a crown of blond hair around a shiny spot of baldness and a patient, even temperament, the man took his time in sketching out Beck.

"Is this close?" he asked when he was finished. He slid his notebook over to her. Alexa, who had taken a snack break next to her mother, peeked over at the drawing.

"That's perfect," Mara said, quickly moving the notebook out of Alexa's line of sight. As if the man could do her harm from it. "You're very good at your job, Walden," she added, thoroughly impressed. He'd even managed to add in the sneer that had pulled up the corner of Beck's lips as he said goodbye.

"I'd always wanted to be an artist, though even I'm surprised that I wound up here." Walden motioned around the conference room but she knew he meant the department as a whole.

"I can understand that," she admitted. "I used to dream of running my own interior design business. Now I work at a flooring company trying to convince people redoing their floors is the first step to a happy home." Mara gave him a wry smile. Walden shrugged.

"Hey, the floors are the foundation of a home. Not a bad place to start at all," he pointed out. Mara laughed.

"You seem to be a very optimistic man. I suppose your glass is always half full?" Walden pushed his glasses back up the bridge of his nose and stood with his notebook.

"It's better to have a half-full glass than an entirely empty bottle." He gave her a nod. "I'm going to take this to the captain now. It was nice to meet you, Mara."

It took her a moment to return the sentiment, as she was slightly stunned by the weight of his previous statement. She wasn't the only one with pain in her life, and compared to most, hers wasn't the worst. Her thoughts went to the teens in the hospital. She looked at Alexa, transfixed by her bag of cereal. At a time when families and loved ones were supposed to be coming together for holidays, Mara couldn't imagine what she'd feel like if she were to get a call like the one the families of the teens were no doubt receiving.

"Knock, knock." Mara shook herself out of such dark thoughts and focused on Cassie standing in the doorway. "Now that you're finished, I've been told to tell you that you don't have to hang around here any longer," she said, all smiles. Her gaze went to Alexa. "I'm sure there are much more exciting places to be than a sheriff's department."

Although Cassie was no doubt being polite, Mara couldn't help but wonder who'd told the woman that Mara should leave when finished. Had it been a polite suggestion to start off with or had the young woman changed the tone to stay nice? Mara mentally let out a long, loud sigh. Feelings of uncertainty, self-consciousness and guilt began to crop up within her again.

And she hadn't even been in Riker County for a full twenty-four hours yet.

Instead of telling the truth—that she'd like to stay until Billy came back—Mara stood with an equally warm, if not entirely true, smile.

"There are a few places I'd like to visit," she tried, attempting to wrangle her child's toys and food back into their appropriate places within her bag. "Plus, it does seem to be a nice day outside."

Cassie nodded, following Mara's glance out of the conference room windows. Every Southerner had a love-hate relationship with winter. South Alabama had an annoying habit of being humid and hot when it should be chilly or cold. Christmastime was no exception. Mara had left her jacket in the car. She doubted she'd need it while in Carpenter, though she wouldn't have minded being proven wrong. At least in North Alabama, where she lived with Alexa, the promise of being cold in time for the holidays was sometimes kept.

"Could you ask the sheriff to call me when he gets a chance?" Mara asked when Alexa and her things were finally ready to go. Cassie nodded and promised she would. Together they walked past the hall that led to the back door and, instead, moved past the offices to the lobby.

It was hard to not smile at the department's attempt at decorating. Colored lights and garlands covered every available inch. On the lobby desk there was even a small Charlie Brown Christmas tree—twigs and a few colorful glass ornaments. An unexpected wave of guilt pushed against Mara at the sight. Not only had she disrupted the life of the sheriff by showing up, but she'd also left behind her own planned Christmas with Alexa back home. Decorations and toys, even holiday treats she'd already baked and packaged. But now that Billy knew about her, what would the holiday look like?

The deputy who had given the news of the overdoses earlier gave them a quick smile while still talking to the secretary, another person Mara didn't recognize. The only other people in the lobby were two women waiting in the chairs.

As she had with Donna Ramsey in the coffee shop, Mara recognized one of them, a woman named Leigh Cullen. Unlike Donna, Leigh recognized Mara right back. She stood abruptly, pausing in whatever she had been saying.

"Thank you again for everything," Mara said in a rush, cutting off eye contact and disengaging from her spot next to Cassie. "See you later."

"You," Leigh exclaimed, loud enough to catch the entire lobby's attention. Mara had the wild thought that if she could run out of the building fast enough, Leigh would somehow forget about seeing her. That she could literally outrun her past. But then Leigh began to hurry over toward them, her face redden-

ing as she yelled, "How dare you show your face here again!"

Mara angled Alexa behind her and braced for a confrontation. One she hoped wouldn't be physical. It was one she deserved but not one she was ready to let Alexa witness. However, Cassie surprised them all.

In all of her compassionate glory, she stepped between Leigh and Mara, and held up her hand like she was a traffic guard telling the driver of a vehicle that they'd better halt their horses. It stunned both women into silence.

"No ma'am," Cassie said, voice high but firm. "You do not act that way in a sheriff's department and certainly not in front of a child."

For the first time, Leigh seemed to notice Alexa on Mara's hip. Still, her eyes remained fiery.

"Don't you know who this woman is?" Leigh continued, though her voice had gone from an explosion to a low burn. Probably because the deputy's attention was fully on them now. "Do you know what she let happen?"

Mara's face heated. Her heartbeat sped up. How had she thought coming back to Riker County wouldn't end in disaster? That someone wouldn't recognize her?

"I know exactly who she is and you don't see me hollering at her like this," Cassie said. Though she'd been polite before, Mara could see her sharp edges poking out in defense now.

"Maybe you should take a breather, Leigh," the

deputy added with absolute authority. He looked confused by the situation but determined to stop it.

"You shouldn't be here," Leigh said. She turned away, grumbling a few more not-so-becoming words beneath her breath, and stomped back to her companion, who'd remained seated.

"I'm so sorry, Mara." Cassie didn't take her eyes off Leigh's retreating back. "I don't know what came over her."

That clinched it. Cassie didn't know who Mara was.

"Thank you," Mara said, honest. "But it's alright. I don't blame her one bit." Without explaining herself, Mara took Alexa and left the department.

It wasn't until they were locked inside the car, "Jingle Bells" playing over the radio, that Mara broke down and cried.

Leigh's husband had been gunned down while trying to stop an armed robbery almost three years ago. His killer had been one of Bryan Copeland's drug dealers. If Mara had tried to turn her father in the moment she found out who he was and what he had done, then Leigh's husband wouldn't have bled out in the convenience store on Cherry Street. Mara knew that.

And so did Leigh.

A HALF HOUR LATER, Mara was letting the laughter of her child soothe her wounds as best it could.

They had gone from the department straight to Anthony's Park. Not as green as it was in the summer, the three-mile stretch of trees, walking paths and recreational spots was located near the town's limits, closest to the city of Kipsy. Because of that fact, Mara had often visited the park when she'd first started to meet up with Billy. They'd sit in the parking lot, huddled in Billy's late father's old Bronco, and try to figure out the best way to stop *her* father and his drugs.

Are you sure you want to do this? I can take over from here. You can go home and I won't ever fault you for it, Billy had said one night. Mara still remembered how he'd looked at her then. Concern pulling his brows together, eyes soft, lips set in a thoughtful frown. Compassionate to a fault, Billy had offered her an out.

And would you go home if you were in my place, Billy?

Despite his lower rank back then, in hindsight Mara realized Billy Reed had always been a sheriff at heart. The resolution that had rolled off him in nearly staggering waves as he'd answered had helped Mara come to terms with her own choice to stay.

No. I would see this through to the end.

Mara smiled as Alexa began to giggle uncontrollably at the sand hill she'd just made. Who knew that *seeing it through* then would have resulted in a daughter.

"You're brave."

Mara jumped at the new voice behind her. Afraid it belonged to Beck, she didn't feel much better when she saw it belonged to another man she didn't know. That didn't stop her from assuming he was into some kind of drug, either. Thin, with red, almost-hollow eyes and stringy brown hair, there was a restlessness about him that kept his body constantly moving. He rubbed the thumb of his right hand across his index finger over and over again but, thankfully, the rest of him stayed still on the other side of the bench.

"Excuse me?" Mara said, body tensing so fast that she nearly stood.

"You're brave to let her play in the sand box," he said, motioning to Alexa. The little girl looked up from her spot a few feet away but lost interest immediately after.

"How so?"

Mara slowly moved her hand to the top of her bag. The playground they were at was out in the open, which made it very easy to see how alone the three of them were now. The man could have looked like George Clooney and Mara still would have been trying to get her phone out without being noticed.

"The sand. It's going to get everywhere," he offered. "I'm sure it won't be fun to clean up."

"I've dealt with worse," she replied, politely. "Plus, she loves it."

The man shrugged.

"I guess you're a better parent than most." He never stopped rubbing his finger, like a nervous tick. It made Mara's skin start to crawl. She opened her bag slowly and reached her hand inside. "So, Mara, was Bryan a good parent?"

Her blood ran cold and froze her to the spot. The man's smile was back.

"Who are you?" she managed. "What do you want?"

He answered with a laugh.

"Let's just say I'm a friend of a friend." Mara's fingers brushed against the screen of her phone. All she had to do was unlock it and tap twice and it would connect straight to 911. But apparently the man had different plans. "If you don't take your hand out right now, I'm going to teach you a lesson in manners in front of your daughter," he said, his smile dissolving into a look that promised he'd carry through on his threat.

Mara pulled her hand out to comply, but she wasn't about to submit to him completely. She stood, slowly, never taking her eyes off him.

"What do you want?" she repeated.

All the fake politeness left him. When he answered his tone was harsh and low. It made the hair rise on the back of her neck.

"Bryan Copeland's drugs and blood money. What else?"

Chapter Six

Her father might have been a lot of things, but Mara had learned a few good lessons from him. Once he'd told her a story about when he was a young man working in a big city. He'd decided to walk home instead of taking a cab, wanting to enjoy the night air, and a man tried to mug him at knifepoint.

Bryan refused to let anyone take advantage of him and used the only weapon he had on him. He took his house keys, already in his hand, and slid the keys between his fingers so when he made a fist, his keys were sticking out, ready to teach his attacker a lesson.

Mara had never heard the rest of the story, only that her father had left that alley with all of his belongings still with him. He would use that story throughout her youth to try and teach her to, at the very least, always keep her keys in her pocket instead of her purse. Because no attacker feared a weapon their victim couldn't get to in time. And usually they didn't care about keys, either.

So as soon as her new friend asked about drugs

and blood money, Mara's hand went straight into her pocket.

"I don't know what you're talking about," she said, pulling her keys out. "I think it's time for us to leave now."

The man shook his head, which Mara expected. Leaving, she gathered, wouldn't be easy, but at least now she had *something* that would hurt him if he got physical. Which she prayed wouldn't be the case. Alexa could still be heard playing behind her.

"You don't leave until I say you leave," the man bit out.

Mara angled her body slightly to hide the hand with her keys. She threaded one between her index and middle fingers and then another between her middle and ring fingers. If he noticed her making the fist, he didn't comment on it.

"My father doesn't have any blood money or drugs left to find," she answered. "And if he does, I'm the last person who would know where they are."

The man seemed to consider her words for the briefest of moments before a sneer lit his face.

"He said you'd deny it."

That made Mara pause.

"Who?" she asked. "My father?" Billy hadn't been the only man in her life she'd not spoken to since she'd left Riker County. She hadn't communicated with her father in any form or fashion since he'd been sentenced. And even then that had been brief.

In the time in between then and the present, had he been talking about her?

"Your friend Beck."

Mara's stomach iced over. She tightened her grip on her keys until they bit into her skin. Apparently Beck worked fast, whoever he was.

"I haven't talked to my father in years," Mara said, trying to keep her voice even. The man behind the bench looked like he would prey on anyone showing fear. Like a shark waiting for blood. "If he has anything hidden, I'm not the one to ask to find it."

"You know, you keep talkin' but I still don't believe you."

He cut his eyes to the space behind her that Mara knew contained Alexa. On reflex, Mara stepped to the side to block his view. The ice in her stomach might have been created in fear but that didn't mean she wouldn't use that to fight tooth and nail to keep the creep away from her daughter.

Maybe the man sensed that. He lazily slid his gaze back to hers and put up his hands in defense.

"Now, I don't have any weapons on me, little miss," he started. "But if you don't come with me I can still make some trouble. For all of us." He dropped his gaze to show he was trying to look at Alexa again. The mistake cost Mara her patience.

"I'm leaving," she said. "If you try to stop me I'll call the cops."

"There won't be any need for that," he replied, his sneer dropping again. In its place was an expression filled with intent. Evil or not, Mara wasn't going to stick around and find out. Mara tried to recall everything Billy had ever taught her about protecting herself in the few seconds it took for the man to round the bench. But all she could think about was a football game she'd watched with her father a few weeks before they'd caught him.

Sometimes the best defense is a good offense.

So, with Billy's voice ringing in her ears, Mara lunged out at the man with her fist of protruding keys. However, Mara's lunge turned more into a stumble. No matter how much she wanted to keep the creep away from her and her daughter, her lack of experience in attacking strange men and the surge of adrenaline through her wasn't helping her. Her fist missed his face but snagged his ear before she lost her footing.

The man let out a strangled cry as one of the keys cut into the side of his ear. Mara tried to steady herself enough to throw another punch that would do more damage, but the man was faster. He grabbed her wrist and squeezed hard.

"You little—" he snarled, but Mara refused to give in. She brought her knee up hard into the man's groin. The hit connected and whatever thoughts he was going to convey died on his yell of pain. He let her go and immediately sank to the ground.

It was the opening she needed.

Mara turned tail and went to Alexa. She grabbed her so quickly that the little girl instantly started to fuss. When Mara started to run toward her car, the little girl went from annoyed to scared.

Maybe she sensed her mother's fear.

Or maybe she heard the man get up and start chasing them.

BILLY WASN'T HAVING a good day.

Though he knew he had no room to complain. Not after he'd seen Jeff Briggs's mother in Santa earrings weeping for her son who was lying in the hospital in a coma. Stanley Morgan wasn't much better than his friend. The doctor had told Billy and Suzy they were certain that Stanley would wake up, they just couldn't say when.

Billy had personally given each set of parents the news once a nurse identified the teens from her neighborhood. None of them had any idea that either boy had been using drugs.

Billy let out a long, loud breath.

"I'm going to call the office to see if we have a good sketch of Beck to work with," Suzy said when they were back to driving.

Billy nodded and turned the morning talk show down as Suzy spoke with Dane. He watched as downtown Carpenter flashed by their windows. It was a warm day, but not as humid as it could have been. Still, Billy wouldn't have minded changing out of his blazer to one of his running tees. His sheriff's star shone on his belt, reminding him that just because it was warm didn't mean he could start slacking in his appearance.

"She did what?" Suzy asked, voice laced with surprise and simultaneously coated with disapproval. Billy turned the radio off. He raised his eyebrow in question but Suzy held up her index finger to tell him to hold on. "Yeah. Okay, I'll tell him," she continued into the phone. "Shouldn't be a problem. Thanks, Dane."

"What was that about?" Billy asked once Suzy ended the call. For a brief moment he wondered if Mara had left town again. This time taking a daughter he knew about.

"Leigh Cullen tried to start something with Mara after she was done with the sketch artist. Apparently Leigh's been saving up some anger for her." The knot Billy hadn't realized had formed in his chest loosened. Mara hadn't decided to run off into the night, or day, again.

"What do you mean, she tried to start something?"

"While Mara was leaving the station, Leigh started hollering and came at her." Billy tensed with a flash of anger. Suzy didn't miss it. "Don't worry, she didn't get far. Deputy Mills and Cassie handled it while Mara went off to take Alexa to the park. At least, that's where Jones said he thinks they were going. He wasn't sure. You know how he is when Cassie's trying to talk to him. His attention breaks a hundred which ways."

Billy couldn't help but let out a chuckle. He had, in fact, noticed how Dane couldn't help but lose some of his concentration when the trainee dispatcher was around.

"You give him such a hard time about her, you know?" he pointed out. Instead of continuing straight, taking them in the direction of the office, Billy was already putting on his blinker to turn. Anthony's Park wasn't that far away.

"And he gave me a hard time when I went out with Rodney a few years back, so I'm still getting even." She gave an indifferent shrug. Billy couldn't argue with that. "So, we're heading to the park?"

"I don't know how serious this Beck person is, but I don't want to take any chances until we catch him, or at least know more. And after seeing those kids laid up in hospital beds, and knowing that Beck showed up at Mara's house and threatened Alexa—" Billy's grip momentarily tightened around the steering wheel. "Well, I'd feel a lot more comfortable if Mara and Alexa stayed a little more hidden while in town." Billy didn't slow down as he took another turn, his sense of urgency growing. "Plus, I have a feeling I'm going to need to have a talk with Mara."

"You want to visit her father," Suzy guessed.

Billy nodded.

"If things start escalating, then I want to talk to the source himself before this thing gets out—"

"Billy!"

Suzy pointed out her window into Anthony's Park to their left. Billy had already been focused on driving to the running trail entrance, what used to be Mara's favorite path to walk, and hadn't noticed the playground or the green expanse between it and the parking lot.

But one look at Mara running with Alexa in her arms and a man chasing them, and a meteor could have crashed down next to them and he wouldn't have noticed.

"Hold on!"

The side road that ran to the parking lot was too far away for his comfort, not when the man was so close to Mara and Alexa, so he cut the wheel hard. The Tahoe went up and over the curb with ease.

"Can you see a gun on him?" Billy yelled, blood pumping as he sped up.

"Not that I can tell," Suzy hollered back.

The man heard the approaching vehicle and turned. Billy was close enough to read the shock on his face. Apparently seeing a Tahoe barreling toward him was enough of a threat to make him rethink his current plan of action.

"He's changing direction," Suzy yelled. "Heading for the walking trail!"

Billy floored it toward the concrete trail that ran through the woods, knowing that once the man broke through the first line of trees the Tahoe wouldn't have enough room to follow. The man, however, was fast. Billy slammed on the brakes as the fugitive slipped between the trees.

But that wasn't going to stop Billy.

He flung his door open and only hesitated a moment to look behind them at Mara.

"Are you okay?" he called, adrenaline bombarding his system. The second he saw her nod, Billy turned and was running. "Stay with them," he yelled to Suzy.

And then Billy was in the trees.

Chapter Seven

The man opted to avoid the only paved walkway that Anthony's Park had to offer. Under normal circumstances that would have been just fine. While there wasn't enough space for a vehicle to drive between the trees, there was more than enough for someone to explore or deviate if you were truly bored with the even, smooth path.

However, chasing someone?

That was a different story.

Billy weaved through the trees, attempting to copy the perp's zigzag route while adjusting his pace to the uneven terrain. At least if the man had a gun, Billy would be able to fall back to cover without much issue.

"Riker County Sheriff, stop *now*," Billy yelled out as he swung around another tree and barely avoided the next. The man didn't even hesitate. "Stop now or I'll shoot!"

That did the trick in breaking the man's concentration.

His foot caught on a tree root and down he went.

Billy was on him in seconds, gun drawn and ready for a fight if needed.

"Don't move," he commanded. "Put your hands on your back!"

The man obliged, but not without complaint. He wheezed and groaned into the dirt before catching his breath enough to mumble out some heated language. It didn't bother Billy. He'd heard worse.

"I didn't do anything." The man finally had the brass to yell as Billy pulled his cuffs out and slapped them on his captive's wrists. The run seemed to have burned him out. The heat wasn't helping matters.

"It looked to me like you were chasing a woman and her kid," Billy said, tugging on the cuffs to make sure they were secure. "And I don't know about you, but to me, that looked like something."

"You don't know what you're talkin' about," the man hurled back.

"Well, good thing I'm going to explain it to you back at the station." Billy secured his gun and helped the man get to his feet. "You run again, or try anything funny, I'll show you just how much more in shape I am than you," Billy warned. The man, covered in sweat, spat off to the side in anger. "And you spit on me or mine, and that's felony assault against an officer of the law. Got it?"

The man grumbled but didn't kick up too much of a fuss as Billy led him out of the woods. Suzy, ever alert, was standing in front of Mara and Alexa, sandwiching them between the Tahoe and herself. Her hand was hovering over the gun at her hip, ready to defend the civilians at her back. When she saw them, there was nothing but focus in her expression.

"I called for backup," she said, not leaving her spot. "Deputy Mills was in the area. Should be here soon."

On cue, the sound of a distant cruiser's siren began to sing.

"You're making a mistake," the man tried again. "I'm the victim here! Did you see what that bitch did to my ear?" Billy kicked out at the back of the man's leg. "Hey," he cried out, stumbling forward. Billy pulled back on his cuffs to keep the man from falling.

"Watch your step there, buddy," Billy said. "Wouldn't want you to hurt yourself."

Deputy Mills came into view soon after. He drove around to the parking lot that looked out at the play-ground and stopped. Billy used his free hand to fish out the keys to the Tahoe he'd shoved into his pocket before.

"Will you take the Tahoe back to the office?" he asked Suzy. "Our friend here can ride with Mills." Billy glanced at Mara. She was rubbing Alexa's back while the little girl cried into her neck. "I'll catch a ride back with you."

It wasn't a question, but still Mara nodded. Her face was pinched, concerned.

"Sounds good, boss." Suzy caught Billy's keys. "I'll go ahead and call Chief Hawser and tell him what's happening. I'm sure he won't mind, though. As long as we get men who like to terrorize women and children off the streets." She cut a piercing look at the man.

"Agreed. Call ahead and tell them to make the interrogation room *comfortable* too," he added, in a tone that let his perp know that his humor was sarcasm only.

"Will do," Suzy said. She was already dialing the department's number. Billy passed her but made sure to angle his body between the man and Mara and Alexa as they passed.

Mara didn't comment as they all walked over to Deputy Mills's cruiser, a few spots down from Mara's car, but Billy didn't miss her soft reassurances to their daughter that everything was going to be okay. It sent another flash of anger through him. When Deputy Mills helped get the man into the cruiser Billy might have been a little rougher than usual with him.

"Read him his rights, deputy," Billy said when he was shut in the back of the car. "And don't let him give you any trouble."

Deputy Mills nodded.

"Yessir."

Billy watched as the cruiser pulled out and away before he went to Mara. She was leaning against the side of her car, still rubbing Alexa's back. The little girl wasn't crying anymore but a few sniffs could be heard. Those little sounds carried a much stronger punch than Billy thought was possible.

"Is she okay?"

"Oh, yeah, she's fine," she assured. "I just scared her a little when I had to grab her and run."

"Tell me what happened, Mara."

"Can we get out of here first?" she asked. Her gaze swiveled past him to the playground in the distance.

"Yeah, we can." Billy tried to search her face for an indication of how she felt. The Mara he knew had been easier to read than the mother standing in front of him. She was guarded. Once again he wondered what her life had been like in the last two years.

"How long have you been here?" he asked. Mara shifted Alexa so they both slid into the back of the car.

"Not long," she said, starting the dance of buckling the toddler into her car seat. Alexa's eyes were red. Tear tracks stained her cheeks. Billy didn't like the sight. Not at all. "Oh, Billy, can you open my bag and grab a wipe or two?" She motioned to the bag she'd put down next to the car. Billy complied, thinking the wipes were for Alexa, but Mara held out her keys to him instead.

"You want me to drive?" he asked, confused.

Mara gave him a small smile.

"There's blood on my keys," she explained. "But if you want to drive, I don't mind that, either."

"You used your keys like Wolverine uses his claws," Billy deadpanned after she'd told him the story of what happened in the park. "I can say that I've never seen that self-defense tactic used in Riker County. Though I guess it was effective."

Mara looked into the rearview mirror and gave him a sly smile.

"Believe me, if I'd had something more useful I would have used it instead."

Billy held up one of his hands to stop her thought. "Hey, it did the trick, didn't it?"

Mara's attention shifted to Alexa strapped into the car seat next to her. She had calmed down in the few minutes they'd been driving, but Mara couldn't help but see the little girl who had cried out as Mara had grabbed her and run. More for her sake than Alexa's, Mara held on to her daughter's little hands.

"It helped us get away, but who knows what would have happened had he caught me." Mara paused. "Actually, I know what would have happened," she said, sure of her thought. Billy kept his eyes on the road but she knew he was listening with all of his attention. "He would have taken me and tried to make me tell him where this fictional stash of my father's is. And when I didn't tell him, he would have used our daughter against me."

Mara had gotten so swept up in her own anger that the words had flown from her mouth without realizing she'd used the word *our*. One little word that had never meant much to her had made Billy react in a very small yet profound way. No sooner had she spoken than his hands tightened around the steering wheel.

"Billy, I—" she started, feeling the immediate need to apologize. Though the car ride wasn't long enough to explain herself or her actions, and certainly not long enough to apologize for them.

"So you think the stash isn't real?" Billy interrupted. There was a tightness to his voice. It caught Mara off guard but she didn't ignore the question.

"I think that guy and this Beck person believe there is," she admitted. "But, really, I can't see how. The investigation into my father's business was exhaustive. Don't you think we—or you and the department— would have come across this cache of money or narcotics? At least have heard a rumor about it?"

In the rearview mirror Mara could see Billy agree with that.

"Still, like you said yesterday, we never were able to fully flush out your father's network," he pointed out. "Maybe that includes this stash."

Mara felt her cheeks heat. She was frustrated and she had a feeling it was only going to get worse. Putting her father in prison should have been the end of this particular brand of headache. And, with some loathing on her part, she realized, heartache. Memories of her childhood filled with a loving father, always watching out for her and taking care of her, tried to break through the mental block she kept up at all times. It was too difficult to remember the good times when she had so thoroughly helped bring in the bad.

"Either way, I don't think it really matters whether or not it's real," she said, hearing the bitterness in her tone just as clearly as she assumed Billy did. "As long as they think *I* know where it is, then Alexa is in danger."

The car slowed as they took the turn into the parking lot of the station. Billy pulled into a staff spot, quiet. Mara wondered what was going on behind those forest green eyes of his. He cut the engine and she didn't have to wait long for him to tell her.

"Well, then, we're going to have to convince them that you don't."

THE MAN'S NAME was Caleb Richards and he'd made a nice little petty criminal career for himself in the past decade. With breaking and entering, convenience store theft, a multitude of speeding tickets and an aggravated assault charge, Caleb's history painted a picture of a man who didn't mind stepping over the line of what was right or wrong. Law be damned.

"That's quite the track record," Billy said to the man after reading his record out loud. They were on opposite sides of a small metal table in the department's lone interrogation room. Behind a two-way mirror sat Suzy and Captain Jones, watching. He'd asked Mara to stay in his office. She might not have admitted it, but her run-in with Caleb had shaken her up more than she was letting on. "And now running from the cops after attempted—what?—kidnapping? That's a bit of an escalation for you, don't you think?"

Caleb's face contorted into an ugly expression of anger.

"Kidnapping? That woman attacked *me*," he yelled. "I was just minding my own business. She should be the one wearing these, not me!" He yanked his hands up as much as his restraints would let him.

"She said you came up to her asking about money and drugs," Billy went on, playing it cool. "In your words, *blood* money. Again, from where I'm sitting that doesn't sound like you were the innocent one in all of this." Caleb shook his head but didn't respond. Which was probably the smartest thing he'd done that morning. Billy pressed on. "Listen, Caleb, Mara doesn't know where the stash is. Despite what Beck tells you, I assure you, she doesn't. I would know," he said honestly. "And I think it's time I tell him that face-to-face. Caleb, where is Beck?"

The man's anger seemingly transformed. Fear registered clearly when he uttered the four words Billy hated in interrogations.

"I want a lawyer."

"This would all be a lot easier if you'd just cooperate with us," Billy tried. "Make a deal and tell us everything you know about your boss and we might take running from a cop off the table."

Billy already knew Caleb wouldn't bite. He was that special kind of stupid criminal, motivated purely by fear. And right now he wasn't afraid of Billy or being charged. Which was more telling than if he'd just stayed quiet.

"I'm not talking until I have a lawyer," Caleb responded. "Got that?"

Billy rapped his fist against the tabletop and smiled. "Got it."

He shut the interrogation door behind him just as Captain Jones and Suzy stepped out of the observation room.

"What now?" Suzy asked, following him as he started to go to his office. He paused long enough to catch Dane's eye.

"I have an idea," he said. "But I think it's time the captain takes a coffee break."

Dane respected, and what's more, trusted Billy, so he decided to play along.

"I've been needing a refill anyways," he said. "And anything that happens while I'm getting that refill, I'll have no knowledge or part of, is that understood?"

"I wouldn't steer you wrong," Billy assured him. Dane nodded and left them outside Billy's office.

"Okay," Suzy said, unable to hide her trepidation. "What's this bad plan of yours?"

Chapter Eight

No sooner had Mara slipped into the interrogation room than Caleb tried to tell her to leave. He was more than surprised when she shushed him.

"Be quiet, you idiot," she said in a harsh whisper. She shut the door quietly behind her but paused to listen for anyone who might have heard. At least Caleb was good at following some instructions. He didn't make a peep.

"I suggest you don't raise your voice," she said, taking a seat in the chair opposite the man. He watched her through a shade of confusion and an even darker shade of mistrust, both apparent in his widened eyes and pursed lips. He hadn't expected to see her, she suspected. Certainly not alone. That was just fine by Mara. She didn't need his trust. She just needed to avoid his suspicion. "The sheriff just stepped out on a call and the rest of them are otherwise distracted, but I wouldn't push our luck by wasting any time."

Mara leaned back in the chair, crossed her arms over her chest and lifted her chin enough to show that she was above the business she was about to discuss. And, by proxy, above Caleb. His round eyes took on more of a slit as he, in turn, tried to size her up. Criminal background or not, Mara knew she was smarter than he was.

"I told you all that I'm not talking until I get a lawyer." He said it slowly, testing her.

"Well, good thing I don't care about all of that," Mara said dismissively. "What I *do* care about is this." She dropped her arms from her chest and jabbed one finger on the tabletop. Not dropping her fixed stare into his beady little eyes, Mara kept her voice clear, yet low. "How did Beck find out about my father's stash when we spent so much time trying to keep it a secret?"

Caleb's reaction was almost laughable. His eyebrows floated up so high they nearly disappeared into his hairline.

"You're saying you do know about the stash, then," he said with notable excitement.

Mara shushed him again for his volume.

"Yes. What do you think I am? An idiot like you? Of course I know about the stash. I'm Bryan Copeland's only child. Do you really think he'd build his own drug empire and *not* tell me? We always knew he might get caught, so he came up with a backup plan. Me."

Caleb's look of surprise morphed into a smugness. He leaned toward her.

"I wasn't buying you not knowing anything," he said, matter-of-factly.

"Glad to know you've got some brains in that head of yours," Mara replied with a little too much salt.

"Hey, you better watch that mouth of yours," Caleb warned.

Mara snorted.

"Or what? You going to magically uncuff yourself and beat me while in the middle of the sheriff's department? Honey, you can't honestly think *that's* a good idea."

Whatever smart retort, or at least his version of one, was about to tumble from between Caleb's crooked teeth stalled on his tongue. Like she'd suspected, Caleb was a small fish in a big pond. If he had been prepared to kidnap a woman and her child for Beck then he was either a very loyal lackey or just one who responded to the confidence of the man in charge.

Or, in her case, the woman.

"Now, here's the deal," Mara continued, lowering her voice but not enough to lose its strength. "I want to know how Beck found out about the stash and, for that matter, who this Beck person is. Because I've heard of a lot of people—a lot of big players—and I promise you I haven't heard his name even once."

There it was.

Clear behind his damp straw-colored eyes. An internal struggle while he weighed his options. To help her image Mara tapped her fingers on the tabletop.

"Don't let my mom jeans fool you," she added. "I'm not this soft, compassionate creature you think

I am. And more than the same goes for my father. So answer me. *Now.*"

"Or what?" Caleb shot back with more bite than Mara had anticipated. If she couldn't sway him to see her, or her father, as more threatening than Beck, then he wouldn't give her any of the information they needed.

"Or what?" she repeated, stalling. "I'll tell you what."

And then it was Mara's turn to have a terrible idea.

BILLY WATCHED THROUGH the two-way mirror in absolute awe as the woman he thought he knew completely and intimately grabbed the front of Caleb Richards's shirt and, in one quick, smooth motion, pulled him down hard. The man was so caught off guard that he didn't even try to shield his face. It connected with the top of the table, making a *whack* so loud it was nearly comical.

"If you don't tell me, my father will figure it out soon anyways and then he'll tell everyone it was you who snitched on Beck," Mara said, sitting back in her seat like she wasn't the cause of Caleb's current pain. He put his elbows on the table so he could cradle his nose. There was no blood that Billy could see, but that didn't mean the man wasn't hurting. "Then you'll have not only Bryan Copeland and his associates gunning for your head, you'll also have this Beck fellow and whoever it is he deals with waiting for you to show up. Jail or not, you'll become a target. And I don't have to spell out what will happen when your boss finally catches up to you." Even from Billy's angle he could see the corner of her lips pull up. "Or do I?"

Caleb let out a volley of muttered curse words but he didn't outright try to fight Mara.

"Damn, she's good," Suzy whispered from Billy's side.

He had to agree.

Caleb took a beat to calm his anger.

"I'm screwed either way, then," he finally said.

Mara held up her finger and waved it.

"You tell me what you know and us Copelands will take that as a sign of good faith," she said, diplomatically. "We'll forget your indiscretion of working for a competitor and may even reward you for being helpful. That is, if you *can* be helpful."

A smarter man would have pointed out that Bryan Copeland was no longer competing for anything. That even though some hardened criminals still had a network outside of their prison cells, Bryan's operation had been thoroughly dismantled. Largely thanks to the woman sitting opposite him, promising him a fictional safe haven. However, Caleb Richards didn't appear to be the brightest of men. Mara had found a spot to put pressure on, and after one more long look at her, he cracked.

"I've only heard him go by the name Beck," Caleb started, not looking at all pleased at what he was doing, but doing it all the same. "He found me in a bar, knew my name and asked if I liked money."

Caleb shrugged. "I said *hell, yeah, I do*, and he said I could make a lot of it if I came and worked for him."

"Doing what, specifically?" Mara interjected. "Grabbing me?"

Caleb nodded and scrunched up his face in pain. He rubbed the bridge of his nose.

"He said he'd already done the hard part of getting you to town. All I had to do was get you to tell me where the stash was and grab you if you didn't. Then let him get the rest out of you."

"Wait, Beck said *he* got me to come to town?" Mara asked, picking up on Billy's own question.

"Yeah, he said he knew if he let you know he was trying to find the money that you'd probably freak out and want to check on it." A grin split his lips. "He tried to follow you last night but got a flat tire. By the time he changed it he couldn't find where you'd gone so *bam* he tells me to keep checking all of your favorite spots in town to wait you out."

Billy felt his anger start to ooze up through his pores and turn into a second skin. His hands fisted at his sides.

"And how would he know my favorite spots? Is he from Carpenter or Kipsy, or is he just blowing smoke and guessing?" Mara's relaxed facade was starting to harden. She was uncomfortable.

"No, I don't think he's from here. He was complaining about the GPS on his phone the other day."

"Then he just got lucky today with guessing I'd go to the park," Mara offered. Caleb shook his head.

"He told me you used to go running there a lot and

probably wanted to show your kid the playground since the sun was shining and all. Though, I guess that was a leap of faith on his part."

"But how did he know that?" Billy asked aloud.

"If he's not from here then how did he know I used to go to the park?" Mara asked a split second later.

"He said his friend knows you. And before you ask, no, I don't know his friend or anyone else he works with, really. I only ever met him at the hotel he's staying at."

"And what hotel is that?"

By God, if Caleb didn't tell her.

A KNOCK ON the door stopped Mara from asking any more questions. Expecting to see Billy or Suzy, she was surprised to find a squat man, sweating in his suit.

The lawyer.

"May I ask what you're doing in here with my client?" the man asked, already bolstering himself up. Mara stood too fast, but recovered with a smile that started with a look at Caleb and ended with the new man.

"Oh, I'm just a friend trying to keep him company until you arrived" was all she said. The lawyer opened his mouth, to protest, most likely, but she was already moving past him into the hallway. It was one thing to pull the wool over Caleb's eyes. It was another to try it with a lawyer.

Mara didn't look back as she walked straight toward Billy's office. The closer she came the more she realized that, while she was happy with the outcome of what she'd just done, something felt off. A lot of Riker County's residents hadn't believed that Mara had been oblivious to her father's dealings. Since it had never been made public that Mara was integral in providing evidence against him, a good number of the general public had assumed she was just clever in how she'd gotten away with avoiding any charge by association. Even though *Mara* knew the truth, she realized now that maybe a part of her didn't.

Maybe there was some side of her that had always known the kind of man her father was. Maybe the person she'd just pretended to be in the interrogation room was the woman she really was, deep down.

Maybe the sweet, compassionate person she portrayed to everyone *was* the cover.

Just like her father.

Mara walked into Billy's office and stopped in the middle. Her heart was galloping and her breathing had gone slightly erratic. She pushed her hands together and twisted them around, trying to physically remove herself from whatever hole she was falling into.

"You did great," Billy exclaimed from behind her. Mara jumped but didn't turn around until she heard the soft click of the door shutting. "I mean, he just opened up and—Mara?"

The warmth and weight of Billy's hand pressed down on her shoulder. Even though she couldn't see his face, she felt his concern through that touch.

When she turned to him, she could feel tears sliding down her cheeks.

"Oh, Billy," she cried.

Billy's expression skirted around deeper concern and hardened. His hands moved to the sides of her shoulders, steadying her. Still, she could feel the warmth of his skin through her shirt. She hadn't realized how much she'd missed it.

"What's wrong?" he asked, lowering his head to meet her gaze straight on. His eyes, a wild green that constantly changed their hue and mesmerized whoever was in their sights, pulled the reluctant truth straight from Mara's heart.

"What if I *am* like my father?"

Mara didn't know if she was looking for an answer from the sheriff or, really, if she even deserved one from him, of all people. But, bless Billy's heart, he gave her one.

Though not the one she expected.

He took a step closer until her breasts were pressed against his chest. The closeness brought on a new reminder. One of her body naked against his. Sharing his warmth until it became their heat.

"You are *not* like your father," he said. His voice had dropped an octave. Its rich new volume surrounded Mara, trailing across every inch of her body like a silk ribbon. She resisted the urge to let her eyelids flutter closed. It had been too long since she'd heard Billy talk to her like that, and it wasn't helping the images already starting to pop up in her mind. The fear of being like her father started to chip away.

But not from his words. It was because the man himself was less than a breath away. If she moved her head up enough she'd be able to meet his lips with hers. Would it be the worst idea she'd had?

No. It wouldn't.

"Mara," Billy whispered, though to her ears, it sounded more like a plea. Mara couldn't find the words to respond, if that's what it really was.

A warm flush started to spread through her body as Billy loosened his hold. Instead of backing away, his fingers trailed down her arms and then made the jump to her hips. The air between them went from fear and concern to something else entirely, charged enough that Mara was left speechless.

That was how it went with the two of them. They only needed an instant for their fire to ignite.

"Mara," Billy repeated. He dropped his head but not his gaze. He angled his lips toward hers and Mara, God help her, finally closed her eyes, ready to feel Billy's lips on hers after two years without him.

But Beck wasn't done with them yet.

The sound of glass shattering ripped away whatever moment they were about to have. But it was the sound of Alexa's high-pitched cry that had them running out the door.

Chapter Nine

The possibility that the sound was something as simple as a cup falling off a table and breaking was quickly dismissed when another crash of glass sounded. This time it was followed by Billy throwing his body into Mara's and pulling her down to the floor. He made a cage around her, his hand flying to the gun at his hip in the process.

"Shooter outside," he yelled. On the end of his words were other shouts from the rest of the department. The empty hallway filled as everyone tried to find the source.

"Shots through the conference room," Billy yelled as a *thunk* split the air.

"Alexa," Mara cried. She nearly broke Billy's hold to go the couple of feet to the conference room door. The room where Alexa had been playing with Cassie. The half wall of glass that made up the interior wall of the room crashed to the hallway floor. Billy's hold was concrete around her. Alexa's continued crying was physically pulling Mara but the sheriff was having none of it.

"Stay here, Mara."

"Alexa—" she tried, but Billy wasn't budging.

"I'll get her."

Mara willed her body to stay still long enough to convince the man she wasn't going to run into the line of fire. The hallway around them was filled with noise as Billy and Suzy barked out orders and relayed information back and forth.

Then Billy was calling out to Cassie, the only person watching Alexa.

She didn't answer.

Billy pulled his gun up high and moved in a crouch until he was in the conference room.

"We need a medic," he yelled as soon as he disappeared from view.

In that moment Mara knew that nothing on earth or in heaven could have kept her from going into that conference room. She mimicked Billy's crouch and was about to rush in when someone grabbed her shoulder.

"Let me go first," Suzy said, brandishing her own firearm.

Mara had enough sense to pause, but no sooner had the chief deputy cleared the door than Mara was in the room.

"Oh, my God!"

The window that looked out onto the street was broken, glass sprinkled on the floor in front of it and on the conference table. However, it was what she saw on the other side of that table that had Mara's stomach dropping to the ground.

Among the scattered LEGOs and books was a blood trail that led to the opposite side of the room, just out of view of the window. There, tucked in the corner, was Cassie, sitting up and bracing herself against the wall with Alexa pushed into the corner behind her.

Even though Billy was at Cassie's side, the injured woman found Mara's gaze and spoke to her.

"She-she-she's o-okay," she gasped.

"Don't talk, Cassie. Save your strength," Billy ordered, tone sharp. He put his hand to the side of Cassie's neck. Blood ran between his fingers.

Mara kept her crouch low as she hurried to their side.

"Get Alexa," Billy ordered. His voice was cold. No doubt helped by the blood he was trying to keep staunched by holding the trainee's neck. Cassie started to move but he stopped her. "Mara can grab her. Don't move."

"Thank you, Cassie," Mara said. She touched the woman's shoulder and focused on her daughter. It was clear Cassie had been shot, yet she still had been trying to protect Alexa. Mara reached over her and grabbed for her daughter. Once the little girl realized who she was, her crying only became more pronounced and large tears slid down her cheeks.

"You're okay," Mara whispered, trying to soothe them both. "You're okay."

"Suzy, take them out of here," Billy ordered as soon as Alexa was pressed against Mara's chest.

"Somewhere with no windows. Don't come back until you have a medic with you."

Billy didn't meet Mara's eyes. Instead, he started to talk to Cassie in low, reassuring tones. The whole scene squeezed at her heart.

There was so much blood.

Suzy led them to the dispatcher's small break room, separate from the one law enforcement used, and set down Mara's bag by the door. She hadn't realized Suzy had grabbed it in the first place.

"Stay here until we know everything's alright," Suzy said.

Mara nodded.

Alexa continued to sob into her shirt.

IT WAS SUZY who came to get Mara and Alexa when everything calmed down. The department was filling with people and Suzy had to take them out the back to her car to avoid most of them. She wouldn't explain what was happening until they were driving out of the lot. All Mara knew was that Billy was on the search to find the gunman, along with Chief Hawser and some of his officers. It wasn't every day that someone was brazen enough to attack a law enforcement department. Even more rare was the reality that the shooter had managed to kill, which was the first bit of news Suzy relayed.

"Caleb Richards is dead. The second shot hit him in the head."

"But how?" Mara was shocked. "He was in the

interrogation room. There's definitely no windows in there."

"The poor SOB had to use the bathroom. He got his lawyer to let him go as soon as he walked in. He was shot in the hallway, right in front of the door."

A chill ran up Mara's spine and then invaded every inch of her. The one place she'd thought was completely safe hadn't been able to prevent a death.

"We think the first shot was meant for Caleb," Suzy continued, not stopping for Mara's thoughts. She looked out the windshield, directing her car through traffic. They'd decided that leaving Mara's car in the department parking lot was a good idea. They'd only paused to put Alexa's car seat in Suzy's. "He meant to shoot through the conference room windows once at Caleb, I'm assuming, but—" Suzy paused and seemed to rethink what she'd been about to say.

"But Cassie had the bad luck to walk by the window when he shot," Mara guessed. She looked in the rearview mirror to the back seat, where Alexa was nodding off. She'd been able to calm the toddler down during the half hour or so they'd been in the break room. Pure white rage streamed through Mara at the thought that someone could have…

Mara stopped her thoughts before they went to the darkest *what if* she could imagine. Alexa had had a terrifying day, but at the end of it she was safe.

"How is Cassie?" Mara had heard when the first responders had carted the woman out but hadn't stepped out from the break room to see firsthand.

She hadn't wanted Alexa to see any more blood than she already had.

"She went into surgery as soon as she got to the hospital. Her sister met her there. Beyond that, I don't know."

Mara felt tears prick behind her eyes. She fisted her hand against her thigh.

"Any idea who the shooter is?"

Suzy's knuckles turned white as she gripped the steering wheel.

"No," she admitted. "But believe you me, the sheriff is sure going to find out."

"Good."

They didn't talk the rest of the way to Billy's and Mara couldn't imagine it another way. When she'd started to work with Billy to help bring down her father they'd kept Mara's involvement a well-guarded secret. Suzy had been the only person in the department who had known from the start. At first, Mara had wondered if Billy's insistence on including the woman was born from a relationship that was more than professional. Now Mara knew Suzy was his best friend.

Suzy is good people, Billy had told her, simply. *I trust her more than anyone. And you should, too. She'll never steer you wrong and will always have your back.*

And that's how Mara knew Suzy knew about Alexa.

"You haven't asked why I left," Mara said when the car rolled to a stop in Billy's driveway. Suzy cut the engine. She'd be staying with the two of them until Billy was back, just in case.

"I assume you had your reasons." Suzy turned to face her for the first time, keys in the palm of her hand. "And to leave a man that in love with you, they better have been really good reasons."

"I used to think they were," Mara admitted, more honestly than she'd meant. Her cheeks flushed in response.

"And now?" Suzy asked. Her expression softened.

Mara didn't know how to answer that. Luckily, she didn't have to.

"Mama," Alexa fussed. "Mama!"

Suzy smiled. The tension in the air dissipated. Now Mara could see the mother in the woman next to her coming to the helm.

"Now *that's* a sound I have to admit I miss," she said. "There might be some uncertainty you're feeling in your life right now but I can promise you this. Enjoy this time of her life because babies surely don't keep."

For the first time since coming to town, Mara forgot about her troubles. The three of them went into the sheriff's house, talking about the joys of motherhood, and the Alabama heat and humidity, and the rising price of gasoline.

Anything other than the current dangers of Riker County.

SOMETIME LATER THAT NIGHT, Suzy left. Mara woke up from her spot on Billy's bed with a start, heart racing and breath coming out in gasps. She threw her legs over the side of the bed and tried to get her bearings. The sound of glass breaking faded away as full consciousness replaced the nightmare she'd been having. That's when she saw the note on the nightstand.

I have to run. Two deputies are outside and I'm locking you in. I set the alarm so don't try to leave because I don't know the code to disarm it if you trip it.
Suzy

Mara put the note back down and looked over at her daughter. The sleeping child with her dark hair framing her face looked like a princess. Tranquil during sleep, unaware of the world around her.

And those in that world who would use her mother's love against her.

Mara leaned over and gave the girl a kiss on the cheek before getting out of bed carefully. Her bare feet touched the same hardwood Billy walked across daily. It made her wonder if any other women had been in his room—his bed—since she'd gone. Surely they had. Billy was a great catch by anyone's standards. Why shouldn't he have taken a lover since? With a sinking feeling in the pit of her stomach, Mara realized Billy could indeed *still* be in a relationship with someone. It wasn't like either one of them had asked about the other's love life. Maybe showing up with his daughter had shocked him enough that he'd forgotten to mention his relationship status.

Mara exhaled until her body sagged. She followed

the once-familiar trail that she'd walked during the five months they'd been together from the bed to the bathroom and turned on the hot water in the sink.

Suzy had grabbed her things from the guesthouse, both of them deciding that it would be easier for everyone to be under one roof. No matter the fact that close proximity and Billy Reed were an almost irresistible combination. Suzy had eaten in the kitchen with them before Mara had been able to go through the task of giving Alexa a bath. After that she'd played with her child until both had fallen asleep. That had been welcome yet unintentional. And Mara knew the sleep that had been easy before would now elude her until she heard from Billy.

The water felt great against her skin, warm and soothing. If she wasn't going to go close her eyes again, she might as well use Alexa's being asleep to freshen up. Mara turned off the faucet and went to the shower. Standing under the water she'd still be able to see Alexa, asleep on the bed in the other room. So, more than ready to wash the day off, Mara opened the door as wide as it would go and quickly undressed.

When she stepped into the water stream, she sighed. Then, just to make sure, she moved the shower curtain to the side enough to peek at Alexa. The little girl hadn't moved from her spot. Not even an inch.

Satisfied, Mara stepped directly under the water. It drenched her hair and skimmed down her back while the warmth wrapped around the rest of her. She tried to clear her mind, but all it wanted was to go back to earlier that day.

And to Billy.

Thoughts alone conjured up feelings of pleasure and desire she'd thought would never come again. They weren't complicated feelings, but when they had to do with their past, how could those feelings be anything *but* complicated?

Then, as if just thinking about the man gave her the power to conjure him up, Mara heard the sheriff call out her name. Guilt flooded through her as she tried to erase where her mind had just taken her. She stepped back and quickly wiped at her eyes.

"In here," she answered, reflexively taking a step back so she couldn't be seen through the gap between the shower curtain and the tub. Billy's heavy shoes sounded outside the door.

"Can I come in?" he asked. Something in his voice snagged on a branch of her concern but she answered all the same.

"Yeah. Just please leave the door open for Alexa." Mara reached out, ready to move the curtain to look at the man, but hesitated. "Is she still asleep?"

There was a pause as he checked.

"Yeah, she's snoring a little."

"Good," she said, glad Billy's entrance hadn't woken the little girl.

They both grew silent, only the sound of water hitting Mara's chest filling the small room.

"I'm sorry for being in your space. I would have asked but you were busy and, well, the guesthouse didn't feel as safe," Mara finally said, unable to keep the quiet going any longer. Every part of her body was on alert. Even more so when Billy didn't answer. "You there?" she ventured.

"Can we talk?" He asked it overlapping her question. Something definitely was wrong. Billy's voice was low and ragged.

Raw.

"Of course."

The sound of plastic running along metal made Mara turn to face the other end of the shower. Billy pushed the shower curtain open enough for him to step over the lip and into the tub.

Mara froze, watching as the sheriff, completely clothed, stood in front of a very naked her.

Billy had seen her naked on several different occasions while they had been together. What was beneath her clothes wasn't a mystery to the man. However, she expected him to at least give her a once-over. Even if she was utterly confused as to why he was standing in front of her in the first place.

Yet Billy's gaze never left her own.

He closed the space between them so fast that she didn't have time to question it. He grabbed her face in his hands and crashed his lips into hers. Heat and pressure and an almost dream-like softness all pulsed between their lips. Mara, too stunned to react, let alone speak, stood stock-still as he pulled back, breaking the kiss. He pressed his forehead against hers and spoke with such a strong sound of relief, Mara felt her heart skip a beat.

"I'm just glad you're okay."

Chapter Ten

The first time Billy ever kissed Mara they'd been in the dining room of his house. It had been a long night of trying to track down a dealer who would decide to flip on Bryan, and Billy could tell the world was weighing heavy on Mara. As he had been bringing in their reheated coffee, he'd caught the woman in a moment she'd been trying to hide.

Elbows on the table, head in her hands, shoulders hunched, and with what must have been a myriad of emotions running up her spine and filling her shoulders, Mara had looked beyond the definition of exhausted. And not just physically.

Billy hadn't known he had romantic feelings for the woman until that moment, though he supposed he'd suspected they were there all along. Seeing her so obviously hurting, he had wanted nothing more than to comfort her. To soothe her wounds. To assure her that, even though things were grim, it didn't mean they always would be. And so Billy had pulled her up to him, kissed her full on the mouth and then, while resting his forehead against hers, told Mara that everything would be okay.

How funny that over two years later, and two rooms over, he'd be doing almost the same thing. Yet this time he was the one who needed strength. Though, admittedly, he hadn't planned on seeking it out fully clothed in the shower.

He'd come into the house without any thoughts in his head of kissing Mara Copeland. But then she'd spoken to him through the shower curtain, just like old times, and everything in him had shifted. What if Caleb had taken her in the park? What if she'd been the one shot trying to protect Alexa? Then he'd looked at Alexa on the bed, snoring soundly, wrapped in a pink blanket with some Disney character or another on it.

When Mara had asked if he was there, Billy hadn't cared about the question. Just the voice asking it. In that moment, he'd only been certain of one thing.

He needed to touch Mara, to feel her. To know that without a doubt she was real and alive and simply *there*.

Now, though, Billy wasn't so certain of himself.

True, moments before he'd all but forgotten the world around them. But now?

He raised his forehead off hers and let his arms fall down to his sides.

"I'm sorry," he said, more aware than ever that he was standing fully clothed in front of a naked Mara. "I shouldn't have just—"

Mara threw her arms around his neck, pushing

her mouth back over his. Any hesitation on his part went down the drain with the hot water. Billy pulled her body against him while deepening the kiss and letting his tongue roam a familiar path. Their lips burned against each other, suddenly alive with a mutual attention that always flamed red hot.

The rest of him began to wake as his hands pushed against her soft, wet skin. Unable to stay still, he turned and pushed her against the wall. Water cascaded down his sides as he deepened the kiss, pulling a moan from her. He suddenly wished he had taken his clothes off *before* entering the tub.

And maybe Mara had the same thought.

She broke the kiss long enough to grab the bottom of his shirt and pull up. It stuck halfway off. Billy moved away from her to do the deed himself. He yanked it off and shucked it somewhere over his shoulder. Mara openly looked over his chest before moving her lips right back to his. She let her hands linger at the buckle of his belt. Soon it, along with everything else Billy had been wearing, was kicked out of the tub until there was nothing but skin between them. Billy hoisted Mara up and against the wall. She wrapped her legs around his waist.

They might have lived separate lives in the last two years, but in that moment, it felt like nothing had changed.

THE HOUSE HAD sounded the same for two years.

Occasionally, it creaked, thanks to the wind, despite having long since settled. Sometimes the branches of the tree outside the guest bedroom scraped against the outside wall. An owl that lived somewhere in the trees away from the house would hoot every so often, while the frogs and insects had a constant rhythm that carried from dark until light. The refrigerator's ice maker and the air conditioner both fussed a little when they came on, too. These were the noises Billy was used to, the ones he heard but never really thought too much about.

However, lying awake in his bed, two new sounds began to mingle with the house.

He turned his head to the right and looked at Mara.

Dimly illuminated from the bathroom light that filtered under the door, Billy could see the woman's face, relaxed in sleep. Her hair was splayed across her pillow like something wild and her lips were down-turned. His gaze stayed on those lips for a moment.

He hadn't meant for anything to happen between them. But once Mara had kissed him, he'd known that he couldn't resist her. They might have a complicated past but there was no denying the two of them were connected by something stronger than simple attraction. They'd started a relationship during an intense investigation because being together without *being together* had been too much for either one of them to resist. They needed skin against skin, mind to mind. They needed each other, even when it wasn't what they needed separately. And it was that need that had given him something unexpected.

His attention moved to the little girl between them. Mara had curved her body toward Alexa, protecting her even when sleeping, while Billy had taken up guard on the other side.

After he and Mara had gotten dressed, Billy had been ready to sleep in the guest room or even on the couch. They both knew that their time together hadn't fixed their time apart. Especially when it came down to the fact that Mara had kept Alexa a secret. However, Mara had been quick to ask him to stay.

If only to make sure Alexa doesn't roll off the bed, she had said with a little laugh. Billy didn't know if she was joking or not, but he took the job seriously.

It *was* the first one he'd been given, after all.

For the umpteenth time since their shower together, Billy couldn't stop the blanket of questions that was being woven around him. Holding in every question he had for the mother of his child. The child she'd kept a secret. Why?

And why hadn't he asked her. Why hadn't he gotten an answer before they'd kissed or before they'd gone further?

Billy knew why.

His body hadn't cared that he didn't have answers to why she kept Alexa a secret or why she'd left at all. All it had needed was to know that Mara was safe and then all it had needed was her.

Still, lying there now, Billy knew he should have asked. Because, even if he didn't like the answer— how could he?—he needed one. Just as badly as he needed to stop Beck.

To protect Mara and his daughter.

Billy's cell phone started to vibrate just as thoughts

of being a father picked back up in his mind. Both dark-haired ladies stirred. As quickly and quietly as he could, Billy got out of bed and took his phone into the hallway.

"Reed," he answered.

"We found Bernie Lutz's girlfriend," Detective Walker said, not wasting time. "After we let her go the other night she apparently jackrabbited to the next county over and got stopped going forty over the speed limit. One of the officers knew we were looking for her so they called up and we got them the sketch of Beck and Caleb. She confirmed Beck was one of the two men who threatened Bernie before he died, but had never seen Caleb."

"At least that's one mystery put to bed," Billy admitted.

"They are going to hold her for reckless driving until they can get the sketch artist back in tomorrow so we can try to figure out who this mystery friend of Beck's is. She didn't recognize any of the men she saw from the database. They warned me it probably wouldn't be until the afternoon that they could get it going, though. Apparently Walden's visit to help us was his last stop before his vacation kicked in."

"Figures," Billy muttered.

He told Matt he'd done a good job and they talked a bit more about everything that needed doing the next day before Billy ordered the man to go get some sleep. He ended the call and figured he should take the advice himself. Being exhausted wouldn't help anyone, especially when he needed to focus.

"Everything alright?" Mara whispered, surprising him when he'd lowered himself back into bed. He stayed on his back but turned to face her. Her eyes were closed and he suspected she wasn't even fully awake. Still, he answered.

"Just found another connection to Beck," he whispered.

"That's nice," she responded, the corners of her lips turning up.

Billy mimicked the smile. It had been a long time since he'd had a conversation with half-asleep Mara.

"We also caught the mayor hooking up with Will Dunlap," he whispered. "It was a pretty big scandal but I got to tase them both, so that was fun."

Will Dunlap was Mara's ex-boyfriend and he'd lived in Kipsy most of his life. They'd stopped dating a year before she'd approached Billy in the bar. Mara had said that she'd broken up with Will because her father didn't like him. In hindsight, Billy wondered if that had meant Will was a really good guy or a really, really bad one. Either way, Will left for Georgia after the breakup and Billy had checked into him in secret over the last two years. Trying to see if he had been working with Bryan, he told himself. But, if he was being honest, Billy had thought maybe Mara had gone to be with him.

Because, again, he still didn't know why she'd left. Pregnant at that.

"Good," Mara answered automatically. "I'm glad."

Billy smirked, satisfied the woman wasn't really coherent, and decided to try and get some sleep instead of continuing to mess with her. The last thing he needed to do was accidentally wake up Alexa, too.

"I missed you, Billy."

Billy froze, waiting for Mara to continue.

But she didn't.

Instead, she reached out her hand and found his, her arm going across Alexa's chest. Neither one of them woke up from the movement. Billy stayed still, eyes wide, looking into the darkness, Mara's hand in his.

Her skin was warm and soft.

Only when Mara's breathing turned even again did he finally answer.

"Once you two aren't in danger anymore you're going to tell me everything, Mara," he whispered. However, he couldn't deny one poignant fact any longer. He dropped his voice even lower. "I missed you, too."

SUNLIGHT CUT THROUGH the curtains with annoying persistence. Mara could only guess that the pervading light was what had woken her. She tried to ignore it and fall back to sleep—because if Alexa was still asleep it couldn't have been past seven—but no sooner had she shut her eyes than she realized it wouldn't happen, for two reasons.

First, the moment she had woken and stared up at the wooden beams that ran across the ceiling, she'd remembered exactly where she was. And what had happened the night before. Even as she shifted slightly in bed, Mara felt the familiar soreness of a night well spent with Billy. Just thinking about him taking her in the shower, both of them riding a wave of raw emotion, made heat crawl from below her waist and straight up her neck.

Second, when Mara turned to look at him, a different kind of pleasure started to spread within her. The sheriff was lying on his back, eyes closed and face relaxed, a sight Mara had seen many times during the time they'd been together. However, what she'd never seen before was Alexa tucked into Billy's side, also sound asleep. His arm was looped around her back, protectively, while Alexa had her face against his shoulder, her wild hair splayed around them both.

Together, the three of them made a family.

Or would have, had Mara not left.

You had a good reason, she thought to herself angrily. *You wanted to keep him safe, happy*. Mara balled her fists in the sheets. Tears pricked at the corners of her eyes. *You made a choice*.

Alexa stretched her arm out across Billy's chest and then gave him a knee to the side, as she usually did when she slept with Mara, but the sheriff took it without issue. In sleep he readjusted the arm around the little girl until both settled back to comfortable positions.

You made a choice, Mara thought again. *But now it's not just you anymore.*

Mara felt her chest swell as the idea of the three of them together flashed through her mind. Was that even possible after everything? Did Billy even want that? Sure, they'd had quite the experience in the shower the night before, but that could be chalked up to the heat of the moment. But one night didn't erase her abandonment.

Two *thuds* from somewhere in the house shattered Mara's thought process.

"Billy," she immediately whispered. She grabbed his arm but didn't wait for him to stir. Trying to be quiet, she threw her legs over the side of the bed and ran to the bedroom door. It was already shut, but she threw the lock. When she turned, Billy was not only awake, but untangling himself from Alexa, trying to get out of bed.

"I think someone is in the house," she whispered, coming to his side. Alexa rolled over to the middle of the bed and blinked up at the two of them as Billy stood. "Wait, is someone *supposed* to be in the house?" Mara asked, realizing with a drop of her stomach that maybe the night before *had* been just their heightened emotions and that Billy could have a lady friend who frequented his place.

"*No one* is supposed to be here but the two of you." It was a relief that didn't last long. Another noise sounded from the front of the house. "Take Alexa and get in the bathroom. Call Suzy." He grabbed his cell phone from the nightstand and handed it to her. Then he opened the drawer and took out his gun. Mara grabbed Alexa, trying not to seem too alarmed. Thankfully, when the little girl first woke up in the morning, she was the calmest she ever was. She yawned and let herself be picked up.

"Mama," she cooed.

Billy was about to say something else when a floorboard creaked in the hallway near the bedroom door. The handle started to turn. Mara remembered the lock was busted. Billy pushed Mara with Alexa behind him and raised his gun.

Mara's heart hammered in her chest. Was Beck brazen enough to break into the sheriff's house or send someone else to do it? Was the intruder there to take Mara? Or maybe find out what Caleb had told them at the station? What if the shooter was just there to clean house?

"I have a gun trained on the door and I won't hesitate to use it," Billy barked out.

Another creak sounded.

"Billy Marlow Reed, if you shoot me and ruin my favorite blouse, so help me I will come back and haunt you!"

Billy instantly lowered his gun but Mara didn't loosen her stance. She didn't recognize the voice. Another creak sounded and soon a woman was opening the door, a hand firmly on her hip.

"Sorry," Billy said, sounding like it. "But next time, Mom, you've got to call before you show up."

Chapter Eleven

What a sight they must have been for Claire Ann Reed.

Billy had a pair of flannel sleep pants on and a white T-shirt, and he had a crazy case of bed hair not to mention a gun in his hands. Alexa was in Mara's arms and sporting equally wild hair and a Little Mermaid nightgown that went to her shins. And Mara? Well, she wished she could have met Billy's mom wearing more than one of his old sports shirts, two sizes too big, and a pair of his boxers. Why she hadn't declined the clothes he'd handed her after their shower and simply grabbed her own out of her bags, no more than two steps from the bathroom, she didn't know.

"To be fair, I *did* call," Claire said with a pointed glare at her only son. "Twice. And when you didn't answer I decided to let myself in. And, to be fair *again*, I'm your mother, it's Christmastime and you should have known I'd come in early!" For the first time she looked at Mara and Alexa. Her demeanor changed from scolding to polite. She smiled. "Now, I have fresh coffee in the kitchen, if you'd like some."

"Fresh coffee? How long have you been here?" Billy asked.

Claire laughed.

"Long enough to slice up some apples and oranges for a healthier breakfast than I'm sure you usually eat." Claire looked at Mara. "Maybe the girl might like some?"

"Alexa," Mara offered. "Her name is Alexa. And she does love oranges."

Claire's smile grew until she looked back at her son.

"Now get dressed and come explain to me why you almost shot me." Her eyes turned to slits. "And why there's no big green tree with ornaments and lights all over it in the living room."

And then she was gone.

Mara and Billy stood still for a moment. Mara's cheeks started to cool. She hadn't realized she'd been blushing. While she knew the woman's name and had heard stories, she'd never met Claire in person. Now the chance at a normal first impression was gone.

"Well, this was unexpected," Billy finally said, moving to shut the bedroom door. He managed to look sheepish. "That was my mom."

"I gathered that," Mara said, putting Alexa down on the bed. Mara dragged her hands down her face and let out a long sigh. "Of all of the times I wanted to meet your mother, it wasn't while I'm wearing her son's boxers."

That got the sheriff to crack a smile.

"At least we had Alexa with us," he pointed out. "We

could have been in a much more…compromising situation."

He was trying to lighten the mood but the comment reminded Mara to ask an uncomfortable question.

"Does she know about us? Or did she?"

The humor drained from Billy's face. He shook his head.

"She knew we were spending a lot of time together but I said you were a friend. I wanted to keep things under wraps during the investigation and trial. She doesn't know you're Bryan's daughter, though."

"Mama," Alexa said again, drawing the word out. She knew what was next but kept her eyes on Billy. They had less than five minutes before Alexa started yelling for num-nums, her favorite phrase for food.

"And how do we explain us?" Mara asked.

Billy put a hand to his chin, thoughtful.

"We don't," he finally said. "Not yet. Not until we figure out what *us* is. And not until we get this Beck situation straightened out."

It was a sobering statement but one Mara took with her chin up.

"Okay," she agreed. "Then I guess I should change."

Billy went to the closet next to the bathroom. Without looking back he said, "You look pretty good to me."

MARA PUT ALEXA in her favorite blue shorts, a flowery shirt with the words The Boss across the front and tried to manage the girl's thick hair into a braid. It was sloppy, at best, but the toddler was hungry and let her mama know quickly she wasn't going to sit still any longer.

"I can take her out there while you get ready, if you want," Billy said after surveying the process in silence. Though he had laughed when he saw what Alexa's shirt said. Mara didn't want the man and his mother to feel burdened by attempting to negotiate with an early-morning Alexa but she also wanted to look decent before she had to sit down across from Claire Reed.

"Good luck, then," Mara said to the man. He smirked. The image sent a jolt through her. Billy Reed looked good no matter the time of day or situation. He was just one hell of an attractive man.

"Alexa, want to come eat with a crazy lady who likes to barge into houses unannounced?" he asked the girl with a slightly high-pitched voice.

"Yeah," Alexa shot back with her own high octaves.

"Then let's get out there, partner!"

Alexa was so excited by having someone seemingly on the same wavelength that she reached for Billy's hand. He grabbed hers without skipping a beat. But Mara saw him stiffen, if only for a moment. She realized that it was the first time he'd held his daughter's hand. As they disappeared from view, Mara couldn't help but feel the weight of guilt crushing her heart.

The sheriff was too good for her.

BILLY WAS HELPING Alexa with her orange slices and Cheerios when Mara came into the kitchen frowning. She'd put her hair into a ponytail and was wearing a white blouse and a pair of jeans that hugged her legs.

Those same legs had been wrapped around his waist last night while hot water ran across nothing but naked skin. Maybe when he'd gone into the bathroom to talk to her he hadn't expected or planned for them to end up having sex.

But that didn't mean he hadn't enjoyed it.

He cleared his throat. Sitting in between his daughter and mother was not the place to be thinking such thoughts. Instead, he focused on Mara's downturned lips.

"What's wrong?"

"I hope you don't mind, but Suzy called and I answered," she said, holding out his cell phone. His mom showing up was enough of a surprise to make him forget he'd left it with Mara. He wiped orange juice off his hand and took the phone.

"Suzy?"

"Billy, we've got another problem," the chief deputy said without missing a beat. "I suggest you go into a room Alexa and your mother are not in so I can use profane language."

Billy stood and held his index finger up to Mara.

"How did you know my mom was here?" he asked. He walked to the bedroom and pushed the door almost closed behind him.

"When you didn't answer, she called me. I told her you should be at home."

"Thanks for that," he said, sarcastic.

"No problem, boss." There was no hint of humor in her tone. Whatever news she had, Billy was sure he wouldn't like it.

"Okay, I'm alone now. Go ahead and get your frustration out and then tell me what's going on."

Suzy took a moment to spew some very colorful words before circling back to the reason she'd called.

"Bernie Lutz's girlfriend is dead."

Billy paused in his pacing.

"Wait, what? How? Wasn't the local PD holding her on reckless driving until the sketch artist could get there? Did they let her go?"

"No."

"But then, how was she killed?" Billy put his hand to his face and closed his eyes. "Tell me she wasn't shot while she was *in* the police station."

"She wasn't."

Billy opened his eyes again and looked at the wall of his bedroom as if it would make sense of everything. It couldn't, but Suzy could.

"Okay, tell me everything and I'll hold my questions until the end."

"I HAVE TO go visit our neighbors in law enforcement," Billy said when he came back into the dining room. He was already wearing his gun in his hip holster, badge on his belt and a button-up shirt beneath his dark blazer. His cowboy hat was even in its position of honor atop his head.

"What happened?"

"Bernie Lutz's girlfriend was supposed to talk to a sketch artist today about the man who was with Beck when he threatened Bernie." Billy went into the kitchen and came back with one of his to-go coffee mugs. "She was in the county over, being held at their police station last night, when a fire behind their building made them evacuate. By the time everything calmed down they realized she was gone."

"She escaped?" Mara asked, surprised.

"That's what they thought. Until a jogger found her a few miles away in a ditch."

"What?" A coldness started to seep into Mara's skin. "So, as far as we know, two of only three people who have had direct contact with Beck have been killed."

Billy shared a look with Mara that she couldn't define. He nodded.

"It looks that way," he said. "I'm going to head out there with Detective Walker to see if we can find anything to help us nail down Beck or his friend."

"Is Beck the man who shot poor Cassie?" Claire asked. She had set down her food to listen when Billy had come in.

"How the heck did you know about Cassie?" Billy asked. "We've been stonewalling the media until we figure out who's doing what."

If Claire was offended by her son's bluntness, she didn't voice it.

"Betty Mills, you know, that nosy old coot who lives in the house behind the Red Hot Nail Salon off

Cherry, called me after she talked to her daughter who has a son who works with you—"

"Dante," Billy guessed.

"I suppose so. Anyways, *he* had the decency to call his mama to let her know he was okay because word got around that two people had been shot, including Cassie, at the department. I figured I'd have better luck communicating with you if I came to town a day earlier instead of waiting by the phone." Claire didn't give her son any room to apologize for not calling her. She turned to Mara. "I was here when Cassie first got accepted as a trainee. She was so nice and bubbly."

Guilt dropped in Mara's stomach. She realized she hadn't asked about the woman's condition when Billy had come home the night before.

"How *is* Cassie doing?" she asked, hoping the answer would ease some of her worry.

"The surgery was a success yesterday, but she hadn't woken up yet by the time I got in last night." Billy's shoulders stiffened. No doubt thinking about one of his own being shot in his domain. "Her sister said she'd keep us updated, though."

"I guess you don't have time to tell me what all is going on?" Claire jumped in. "And why this Beck person seems to be killing everyone he meets?"

This time it was Mara who stiffened. Billy didn't miss it. His frown deepened.

"I don't want you to leave this house," he ordered. "Two deputies are already on the way, including Dante Mills. They'll be watching the front and back of the house and will check up on you every half hour." He looked to his mother. "Mom, I can't make you do anything, but I would really appreciate it if you stayed here. If Mara wouldn't mind, she can go over what's happening with you, as long as you don't tell anyone else. Not even Betty Mills, okay?"

Claire sat up straighter, if that was possible, but she nodded, her short bob of hair bouncing at the movement.

Billy walked over and kissed the top of Alexa's head. He hesitated before leaving the room. Mara knew then that Billy Reed was already 100 percent in love with his daughter. Leaving now would be impossible. Even if Billy didn't want Mara to stay.

She sighed. There were bigger issues to contend with.

For instance, Claire was staring daggers at her.

"He's scared someone will hurt you two," Claire guessed. "Why?"

Mara looked at Alexa and felt fear clamp around her heart.

"Because now I'm the only person we know of to have direct contact with Beck, who is still alive."

CLAIRE WAS A LOT like her son. Or perhaps it was the other way around. The older woman listened patiently as Mara told her everything that had happened, starting with Beck visiting her house. One detail Mara didn't include, however, was her past relationship with Billy. And that Alexa was his daughter.

"So, this Beck man wants you alive because he needs you," Claire said when Mara finished. "At least that's a silver lining, considering he seems to have a friend keen on killing."

Mara couldn't help but agree.

"As sad as it is to admit, yes, there's that."

Claire drained the rest of her coffee from the cup and looked at the toddler across the table from her. Alexa crunched on her Cheerios and became transfixed by a cartoon about pigs Mara had playing on her smartphone. While watching television wasn't exactly a tradition at their house, sometimes it was the only way for Mara to distract the girl.

"So, you came back to town to tell Billy, since he was in charge of the case against your father and is now the sheriff," Claire spelled out. Mara nodded. "And I'm guessing you also told him that Alexa is his daughter."

Mara froze, coffee cup hanging in midair.

"Excuse me?" she said, trying to recover.

Claire actually smirked.

"Any mother worth her salt is going to figure out when she's looking at her grandchild, especially when the little girl has the exact same eyes as her son," she started. "Not to mention, you don't strike me as the type of woman to let your daughter—and you for that matter—sleep in a bed with a stranger. Am I right?"

Mara didn't know what to say, so she answered in a roundabout way.

"I was the one who helped Billy build the case against my father when he first took it over. During that time we…became close," Mara admitted. She paused, trying to figure out what she wanted to say next but found the words weren't coming.

Claire's smirk softened into a small smile. She held up a hand in a stopping motion.

"Listen, my husband was a very private man and I know Billy has picked up that trait," she began. "I've learned a thing or two about respecting his decisions. Because, in the end, he usually has a good reason for everything he does. I'm going to extend that courtesy to you, too, because my son doesn't pick his company lightly. So, I'm going to assume you are a good woman. And a strong one at that, considering what you must have gone through with your father," Claire continued. "But, you coming back here lets me know that at one point you left. And while my son can keep a secret, I know he wouldn't keep one about having a daughter from me for too long." Claire reached over and took one of Mara's hands in hers. "I won't ask you why you didn't tell him about her until now, but I don't want you to sit here and deny that Alexa's my granddaughter, okay?"

Mara, despite the decision she and Billy had made to wait to tell Claire, gave a small nod, unable to look away from the woman. As if she was caught in a trance. Claire squeezed her hand before dropping it. She leaned back in her chair. She still wore a pleasant, warm smile.

"Now, if I wasn't sure you loved my son, I wouldn't be this nice," Claire tacked on. It was a startling statement that instantly got a reaction.

"Love your son? But I—" Mara started, heat rushing up her neck. This time she was interrupted by Claire's laughter.

"Don't you try to deny it," she said, wagging her finger good-naturedly. "The girl's name is proof enough you loved my son—once, anyway. And, if I had to guess, proof that you always intended to tell him about her." She shrugged. "At least, that's my feelings on it."

Mara felt the heat in her cheeks intensify. But this time she too smiled.

"Her name?" Mara asked, though she knew it was pointless. Claire Reed seemed to pick up on things quickly. Much more so than her son. She would have been a phenomenal sheriff.

"Alexa, after Alexander. Which is my late husband's name and one of Billy's favorite people in the entire world." Claire's smile widened. "You named her after her grandfather, didn't you?"

Mara couldn't help it. She laughed out loud.

"Do you know that Billy hasn't even mentioned that yet?" Mara knew it was no use denying the connection between them all. "I thought it would be one of the first things he asked me about but, no, he hasn't said a word!"

"Well, my Billy might be a lot of good things," Claire said. "But, bless him, that boy can sometimes be just plain oblivious to what's right in front of him, too."

Chapter Twelve

"How in the world did she slip away without anyone noticing?"

Billy looked over at Detective Matt Walker in the driver's seat. They'd spent the morning talking to officers and witnesses to the fire, trying to figure out what had really happened. So far, no one knew anything other than that Jessica had been there one moment and then, the next, she was gone.

"Incompetence on the officers' behalf?" the detective asked. "The fire wasn't bad enough to require all of their attention, especially since the fire department was a few doors down, and yet they still managed to lose someone in their custody."

Billy wanted to say no, because everyone he had met that morning had seemed, well, competent.

"A suspect was killed, not only in custody at our department but *inside* of it," Billy pointed out. "Whoever is behind this, whether it's Beck or his friend, they seem to have a skill for avoiding detection."

"The hotel being a good example of that," Matt said.

Billy nodded. He hadn't gotten the chance to tell

Mara yet, but the hotel room where Caleb had said he'd met Beck had been searched.

Thoroughly.

They'd found nothing. Just a cash payment for six days, starting the week before, under John Smith, of all names. The hotel manager and staff had been told to call if there were any more check-ins or sightings of Beck. Discreetly.

"I should have brought more coffee," Billy finally said, massaging the bridge of his nose. "This case is giving me one of those headaches that feels like it will never go away. I've lived in Riker County my entire life and you've been here for years. How is it that two people who've never been here are navigating our home turf so well?"

"Beck's friend could be a local."

It was a thought that Billy had already discussed with Suzy. And one he hated to entertain. Though just because his love for his town and the area surrounding it was great, that didn't mean everyone else saw Riker County with the same fondness.

"If Bryan's so-called stash is in fact real then knowing where it is would help clear everything up, or at least give us a better chance at stopping this guy," Matt continued. "We could use it to bait Beck and end this mess."

Billy sat up straighter. But then he thought about Mara and her body against his, and how much he would hate it if something happened to her or to Alexa.

They'd have to use Mara for any baiting plan to

work. That's why Billy hadn't put much stock in that plan yet. He didn't want her to be in any more danger. They'd just have to figure out a way to pull it off with Mara and Alexa out of harm's way.

Finally, Billy balled his fist.

"I need to talk to Bryan Copeland," he admitted. "*That's* what I need to do. Get him to tell me where the hell this stash is if it's real."

"You think he'd tell you anything, though?" Matt asked. "Considering you're one of the reasons he's in prison?"

Billy shrugged.

"I'll just have to be persuasive."

"You think he'd tell Mara?" Matt ventured with notable caution in his tone. While Billy hadn't told the man about his relationship with Mara, he knew Matt was a good detective. Billy hoped no one else suspected a personal connection between him and Mara. Because, if they did, that meant Beck could possibly know, too. If it hadn't been for the storm the night Mara had shown up, he could have followed her straight to his house.

Just the thought made Billy even more anxious. His phone ringing with the caller ID for Mara didn't help.

"Reed," he answered.

"Billy, it's Mara."

"Everything okay?"

"Yeah, we're fine," she said quickly. Then her voice dropped to a whisper. "Billy, do you think you could come pick me up?"

Her tone made him hesitate. He cast a quick look at Matt, wondering if he should also be quiet.

"Why? What's going on?"

There was movement on the other side of phone. A door shut.

"I think I know where Dad's stash is."

"A MAN NAMED Calvin Jackson was a very unhappy man in the state of Washington who, almost a decade ago, decided to use a local high school's basement as his own personal meth lab," Mara said from her spot at the table. Billy stood at its head while Matt and Suzy were across from her. All eyes were focused as she spoke. "No one would have probably caught him had the lab not exploded—taking Calvin with it—because no one expects a meth lab to be underneath Honors English.

"That's what my father said after we saw it on the news," she continued. "He said if you ever want to hide, you do it not in the last place someone would look, but the last place someone would even associate whatever you are doing with. He said Calvin Jackson had the right idea, just not the right approach." Mara let out a quick breath. "I should have realized then and there that something was off about him, but you know. I just didn't."

Billy fought the urge to put his hand over hers. They might have shared a lot in the last twenty-four hours, but since Mara had called they had fallen into a more professional rhythm. Plus, Mara had left right when Billy had thought things between them were going great two years ago. Maybe chalking up their night together as a one-time nod to their past—and their lack of control when the other was around—would give them a chance at sharing a civil future. One where they could be friends.

One where she wouldn't leave and take their daughter with her.

The thought of never seeing Mara or Alexa again made Billy almost physically uncomfortable.

"So when Mom got out my high school yearbook from the attic, it reminded you of that," Billy guessed. He didn't miss the smile in her voice or the fact that she didn't deny his mother had done just that.

"Yes, it did."

Hiding a stash of money and drugs in a high school had seemed a far-fetched notion until Billy had remembered the school had been completely renovated almost three years ago after a series of storms that had taken their toll.

And that Bryan Copeland had been at the ribbon cutting when the addition had been unveiled.

Mara had remembered that detail because she said she'd been tickled to see her dad on the news, even if he had been in the background. It was the best lead they'd had so far. Even if that didn't automatically mean the stash was hidden somewhere on the grounds.

"But where could he have hidden it without anyone noticing?" Matt asked after Mara was done.

"Well, as far as I know, there's no basement," Billy said, trying to recall the layout. "Then again, I've been told it doesn't look like it did during my high school days. I haven't been there in years. If Bryan *was* going to try to sincerely hide it where no one but him could reach it, he could have used the construction as a way to do just that. And it meets the timeline of when the investigation started to get going. He could have used the storm as an opportunity to make his own personal fallback plan."

Suzy nodded in agreement and then cringed.

"So I guess this means we're going back to high school?"

Billy cracked a quick grin.

"I guess it does."

After several calls made by all three members of his team, Billy went back to standing at the head of the table. This time with a plan.

"Here's the deal," Billy said to the group. "Matt, I want you to keep your attention on finding Beck and his helper or helpers. Because at the end of the day, even if we do find the stash, that doesn't mean our problems with them are over. Work the local angle. If someone we know is feeding this Beck information, we need to plug that hole quick. Talk to the local PD again. See if they have anything to help us."

"Got it," Matt said. "I think I might already have a good spot to start looking."

"Good." Billy looked at Suzy. "Suzy, I want you to come with us, because three sets of eyes are better than two."

Suzy crossed her hands over her chest.

"And?" she asked.

Billy let out a long breath.

"And I hate dealing with Robert by myself," he admitted.

"Robert?" Mara asked.

Suzy was quick to answer.

"The principal. He's something of a chatterbox."

"Which wouldn't be bad if he wasn't always talking about nonsense," Matt added.

"But we need him unless we want to wait for a warrant, which might leak to the public what exactly it is we're looking for," Billy pointed out. "Plus, if we're going to search the high school for a cache of drugs and blood money it only feels right that the principal is at least on the premises."

CARPENTER HIGH DIDN'T look like the school Billy remembered.

Its once-stained, shabby and seen-better-days structure was cleaner, brighter and nearly pristine.

One of the last places anyone would look for a stash of drugs and blood money.

Billy followed Suzy into the staff parking lot, where a man was standing next to an old Mazda.

"Is that Robert?" Mara asked from the passenger's seat.

Billy nodded.

"And we're going to let Suzy distract him while we conduct our own search," he said. "Because I can stand a lot of things, but there are some people on this earth I believe were put here just to test our patience."

Mara laughed and soon they were standing across

from Robert. He was a short man with a crown of dark hair that had a shiny bald spot in the middle. His gut used to extend past the belt and dress khakis that he habitually wore, but he was much slimmer than he had been the last time Billy saw him.

"New diet," he said, looking straight at Billy. He patted his stomach. "Mama said I wasn't getting any younger and told me it was now or never to take control of my life. Health included." He sent a wayward wink to Mara at Billy's side. "She really just wants me to settle down and give her some grandbabies. I said one thing at a time, Ma!"

Mara gave a polite little laugh.

Suzy cleared her throat. "We're kind of in a hurry, Robert," she said, taking a step forward so that his attention stuck to her. "You understand what we're here to do? And why only you can help us, right?"

Robert, feeling the weight of importance on his shoulders, puffed out his chest and straightened his back. His playful smile turned into a determined crease.

"Yes, ma'am." He made a grand gesture and swept his arm toward the front entrance. "I'm ready when you are."

Billy could tell Suzy was holding back an eye roll, just as he could tell Mara was trying not to laugh, but soon the four of them were heading up the walkway.

"Did you really tell him what we were looking for?" Mara whispered when Robert got out his keys. Since it was a Saturday, he'd promised no one else would be inside during the day.

"That we had reason to believe that harmful substances could have been hidden on the premises and we'd like to take a cursory look on the down low before causing a panic."

"And he just agreed to that?"

Billy shrugged. "He'd rather be sure before he subjects his school to good ole small-town scrutiny."

"I can't blame him there," Mara conceded.

Robert opened the door and they all stepped into the lobby. Like the outside, the inside looked much nicer than the school Billy had attended. Still, he inhaled and couldn't help but feel a twinge of nostalgia. The urge to tell the story about a fifteen-year-old Suzy giving Kasey Donaldson a black eye for saying she shouldn't be allowed to play capture the flag because she was a girl was almost too great to resist. Especially when Billy realized the principal's office was still straight ahead, next to the stairs that led to the second floor. He'd watched Suzy do several marches into that office with her chin held high.

Hell, he'd done a few himself.

"Okay, why don't we split up to make this faster," Billy said, shaking himself out of his reverie. "Suzy, you and Robert take the gym and detached buildings, and we'll search the first and second floors of the main building."

Suzy didn't even bat an eye at being paired up with Robert. By the hard set of her jaw, Billy saw that she was in work mode. They had a problem that needed to be solved.

Finding Bryan Copeland's stash would solve it.

Robert followed Suzy, already babbling about something, while Mara turned her attention to him.

"You know, in movies, it's usually a bad idea to split up," she mused.

"Stick with me and you'll be alright, kiddo."

Mara was quick to respond with a wicked grin. It made Billy feel a lot of things he shouldn't be feeling. Maybe they should be splitting up, after all.

IT WASN'T UNTIL they made it to a second-floor classroom that the idea of *them* pairing up showed itself to be a bad one.

Mara noticed a panel of ceiling tiles that were painted a different color than the many others they'd already seen. Since their motto was to leave no stone unturned, she pulled a table over and stood on top of it. She wasn't short, but she wasn't the tallest woman, either. She pushed one tile up but she couldn't see inside the ceiling. She needed just a little more height.

"Billy, get up here and look."

"I don't think so," he said seriously. "I'd snap that table in two."

"Then—"

"It's probably not the best idea for me to get on those chairs, either. Donnie Mathers tried to jump from one to the other in tenth grade and one broke from under him. Broke his arm, bone sticking out and everything." Billy shook his head. "But what I can do without breaking anything is hoist you up."

"Then how about we nix the table and chairs. You're certainly tall enough to be better than a table."

Mara didn't wait to be invited to him. She jumped down and stood in front of him expectantly.

"Just like the time I helped you get that branch that was hanging off of your roof," she said. When he hesitated, Mara feigned offense. "Unless you think I'm too heavy to pick up."

"Don't even pull that," he said, but it got the job done. He wrapped his hands around her and hoisted her up until she was able to move a tile.

"A little more," she said, trying to keep her mind on the task at hand and not *Billy's* hands. He was quiet but adjusted to give her a little more height. It always amazed her how strong Billy Reed was. Mara brought her phone up and shone the light around inside the ceiling.

"Nothing," she reported, not surprised. "At least we looked."

Mara braced for Billy to let her down fast but, instead, he lowered her slowly. Like molasses crawling down a tree, her body slid against his until her shirt caught on him. It had dragged the fabric up to expose her bra by the time her feet were back on the floor. She moved to pull it down, but Billy caught her hand.

She felt her eyes widen and her breath catch. The heat of his hand burned into her skin, but it was his stare that almost set her ablaze. It pierced through the few inches of space between them, and frightened and excited her more than she wanted to admit. Mara couldn't read what the man was thinking.

She sure found out.

He dipped his head down until his mouth found

her own. But it was his hand that surprised Mara. While his tongue parted her lips, his hand let go of hers and traveled down to the cup of her bra. She let out a gasp as he thumbed her nipple until it hardened. It wasn't the only thing. She could feel Billy's arousal as he used his free hand to pull her flush against him.

It was fuel to their already burning fire.

Mara grabbed his belt and pulled the man closer, trying to show him she wanted him just as much as he wanted her. Right then. Right there. However, Billy surprised her by breaking their kiss. His hand dropped away, leaving her exposed skin cold.

Billy met her gaze.

Those green eyes spelled out one word to her.

Regret.

"I-I'll check the rooms at the other end of the hallway," she said, tugging her shirt down quickly. Before Billy could stop her, Mara rushed from the room.

But, with a heavy heart, she realized he didn't even try.

Chapter Thirteen

Mara opened her eyes and tried to make sense of what she was seeing.

Her head pounded and her side lit up in pain. She sucked in a breath and regretted how much it hurt. She tried to move, if only to distance herself from the physical discomfort on reflex, but realized with panic that she couldn't. Her eyes swiveled down to the object pinning her to the ground.

It was a set of metal lockers.

But why were they on top of her? And where—

Then it came back to her.

Mara moved her head from side to side to try and see the rest of the storage room behind her. Except for more lockers and cleaning supplies, she was alone.

She turned her attention back to the weight keeping her against the floor. Tentatively, she pushed her shoulder up to try and free one of her arms. Pain shot fast and hard through her side again but she managed to get her left arm free.

Mara hesitated as footsteps pounded the tile outside the closed door. Someone was coming toward it.

Fast.

Mara put her left hand under the top part of the locker across her chest. She started to push up just as the door swung open.

"Billy," she exclaimed in profound relief.

The sheriff's eyes widened in surprise and then almost immediately narrowed. He came around to her head.

"What happened? I heard you scream," he said, already putting his hands under the top of the locker.

"I'll tell you if you get this off me," she promised, readying herself for the weight to be lifted. A part of her was afraid to see the extent of the damage done to her. She just hoped nothing was broken.

"Alright, get ready."

Billy pulled up and soon the locker was hovering over her. Mara didn't waste any time. She rolled over onto her stomach and dragged herself across the tile between Billy's legs. The pain she'd felt before nearly bowled her over at the movement.

"I'm out!"

Mara turned back to watch the lockers crash to the ground. The noise rang loudly through the room and into the hallway outside. She'd been gone from Billy's side for less than ten minutes. It had been more than enough time for trouble to find her.

"Get your gun out, Billy," she said, a bit breathless. Bless the man, he didn't hesitate. He unholstered his gun, kept his back to the wall and crouched down next to her.

"Someone pushed those over on you?" He motioned to the lockers.

Mara nodded.

"I was looking in them and heard someone walk up. I thought it was you but the next thing I knew I was waking up on the floor under them."

Billy said a slew of curses that would make his mama angrier than a bull seeing red and pulled his cell phone from his pocket. He must have dialed Suzy, because she answered with an update already going, loud enough for Mara to hear. They hadn't found anything yet in their search.

"Suzy, someone's here with us. Tell Robert to lock himself in a room and you come up to the main building pronto. We're on the second floor."

"Want me to call in some—"

The unmistakable sound of gunshots rang through the air. Mara heard it through and outside of the phone. Billy stood so fast she couldn't hear whatever it was that Suzy yelled.

But she knew it wasn't good.

"Suzy?" he called. "What's happening?"

She didn't answer but another gunshot sounded.

Billy cursed again and pulled the radio from his belt. He called for backup using a tone that absolutely rang with authority. It inspired Mara to get to her feet, though it was a struggle.

Acute pain that made her inhale lit up her side— or, more accurately, her ribs. If she hadn't broken any, she'd at least bruised them something mighty. No other part of her seemed worse for wear. Not even the knot on the back of her head where she'd hit the floor.

The moment Billy had finished his call, he turned to Mara. Surprise was clear on his face.

"I'm fine, let's go," she yelled, waving him toward the door.

He didn't wait to argue with her. Instead, he tossed her his cell phone and then whirled back around, gun drawn.

"Stay behind me," he barked.

Mara had no intention of doing anything else.

They left the supply closet and, when Billy was convinced the coast was clear, moved down the hall, heading for the set of stairs at the end.

The second floor of the school was two wide hallways in an L-shape with classrooms lining both sides. The stairs were where the hallways converged and Mara had marched by them when she was fleeing from Billy minutes before. She'd been so embarrassed, and filled with shame and loathing and a hundred other emotions, that she'd gone to the farthest room she could find. She should have been more careful, or at least cautious, but no one should have known about their search other than Matt, Suzy, Robert and a few deputies who'd been ordered on standby.

They should have been alone in the school.

Another shot rang through the air. This time, Mara didn't hear the echo come through the phone. This time, the call ended. A cold knot of worry tightened in Mara's stomach for the chief deputy and the principal.

Billy quickened his steps, moving with his gun

high and ready. Mara sucked in a breath and started to follow when the sheriff stopped so quickly she nearly ran into his back.

"What—" she started, but Billy cut her off.

"Listen," he whispered.

Mara froze.

The unmistakable sound of footsteps echoed up the stairs from the first floor. Someone was coming. And by the set of Billy's shoulders, Mara knew it probably wasn't a friendly. Without turning his back to the stairs the sheriff began to backtrack. Mara gasped as the quick reversal made the constant thrum of pain in her side triple.

The footsteps stopped but Billy didn't.

He kept moving until they were off the stairs.

"Go hide," he ordered, voice low. He nodded in the direction of the part of the second floor she hadn't explored. But she wasn't about to question him.

"Be careful," Mara whispered. She tried to be quiet as she moved as quickly as she could toward the classrooms at the end of the hallway. She chose the middle of three and turned in the doorway so she could still see Billy.

He was looking at her. With a quick jerk of his head he motioned for her to get inside the room. So she went, leaving the sheriff alone.

THE BULLET GRAZED Billy's arm, but it was the man lunging at him that made him lose his gun. It hit the tile and skidded away while his back connected with a wall. Billy took a punch to his face as the infamous Beck snarled, "Where is it?"

Billy pulled his head back up and slung the man off him. If Beck hadn't shot half a magazine at him as soon as he'd seen Billy on the stairs, forcing the man to take cover long enough so Beck could run up, he wouldn't have had the chance to question Billy. Let alone lunge at him.

Blond hair cropped short against his scalp, blue eyes that held nothing but hatred for Billy, and the thin, drawn face of a man who looked to be in his late thirties, all wrapped in a pair of khaki slacks and a collared shirt, Beck didn't look nearly as threatening as Billy had imagined. Certainly not a man trying to create another boom in the drug industry of Riker County.

But neither had Bryan Copeland.

Billy knew that bad men didn't have just one look. Bad men were just men who did bad things. Whether one wore a suit or a wifebeater, it didn't matter.

While Beck tried to regain his balance, Billy threw his own myriad punches. One connected with Beck's jaw, another with his ribcage. The latter blow pushed his breath out in a wheeze but he didn't go down. Instead, he used Billy's attack against him. Bending low, Beck rammed his shoulder into Billy's stomach, throwing him back against the wall.

"Where is it?" he roared again. Beck's anger was getting the better of him. The man took the time to rear his fist back, like he was winding up for the big pitch.

It gave Billy time to bring up his own fist. Hard. It connected with Beck's chin with considerable force. The man made a strangled noise and staggered backward. He held his jaw with both hands. Billy didn't waste time watching what he did next. He turned to look around for his gun.

It lay beneath a water fountain a few feet away.

Billy was running for it, already mentally picking it up and swinging it around on Beck, when he registered a new noise. Footsteps, coming fast.

Could Mara have tried running up to help?

But it wasn't Mara.

He turned in time for something to slam against his head.

Then everything went dark.

"Where's Billy?"

Matt Walker stood in the doorway, a frown pulling down his lips. Sirens sounded in the distance.

"He's okay, but—"

"But what?" Mara walked past him, pain be damned.

"Mara, I need you to stay, just in case," Matt tried, but she was already looking for the sheriff.

"Billy!"

Billy was on the ground. Sitting up, but still, on the ground. He had a hand to the back of his head. His face was pinched. He was obviously in pain.

"I'm okay. Got caught by surprise. Apparently Beck's friend is here." His gaze shot to her side. Mara realized she'd been clutching it. The pain kept intensifying the more she moved.

"Bruising, that's all," Mara said. "What happened out here?"

"I turned my back on the stairs and I shouldn't have." Billy looked to Matt. "One minute I was fighting him and then the next I got slammed with something. Then I could hear the sirens. Beck and his buddy must have run."

"Did you pass out?" Mara asked, worry clotting in her chest. She put her hand to the spot Billy was holding to inspect it closer. There was blood.

"For a second," he said dismissively. The detective must have cleared the other rooms down the hallway she'd been hiding off and jogged back to them. "Matt, Suzy should be outside at one of the buildings. She had Robert with her. Someone was shooting at them."

Matt nodded and grabbed his radio. He told everyone who was listening to keep their eyes out for two suspects and to find Suzy. Apparently he had no intention of leaving Mara and Billy. She was glad for the detective's company. Billy wasn't looking too hot.

"Don't move," Mara chided when he tried to stand.

Billy, of course, tried anyway.

Mara rose with him, hands out to steady the sheriff if needed.

"I'm fine, I promise," he said, swatting at her. As soon as his hand cut through the air, though, he started to sway.

"Billy," Mara exclaimed. She grabbed his arm and gasped at the pain from her ribs.

"You *both* need seeing about," Matt said.

"I'm *fine*," Billy tried again. He steadied himself. The hand he'd had against the back of his head was red with blood. Mara pointed to it.

"That isn't fine, Billy."

He shook his head a little, trying to be dismissive again.

"I just need to take a seat—" he started. But then the man tipped backward.

"Matt," Mara squealed, trying to keep Billy from hitting the tile floor. Matt was fast. Between the two of them they managed to stop the sheriff's fall. They eased him back down to the tile as gently as they could.

"He's unconscious," Matt said, reaching for his radio again. However, before he could call anything in, a voice was already yelling into the airwaves.

"We need a paramedic!"

Chapter Fourteen

The ER nurse was brisk when she told Billy he had a concussion and needed to take it easy. At the very least, for the rest of the day.

"I have a job to do," he objected, already slipping his badge back on. His cowboy hat soon followed.

"So do I," she retorted, her brows drawing together. The effect made her look severely disapproving. "And it's to tell you that you need to rest. Sheriff or not, you're just as human as the rest of us."

Billy was getting ready to harp on the fact that he was a human *who happened to be* a sheriff when Matt walked around the privacy curtain. He gave a polite nod to the nurse who, in turn, smiled.

"I'll go check on my other, less stubborn patients now," she said before throwing Billy a parting look of annoyance. Then she turned to Matt. "I'm going to tell you what I told him. He needs rest."

"Yes, ma'am," Matt responded, dutiful. Billy rolled his eyes.

She pulled the curtain back again so they were out

of sight of the rest of the nooks that lined the emergency room. Thankfully, it wasn't crowded.

"I thought everyone was supposed to love the sheriff," Matt said with a smirk the moment she was gone.

Billy shrugged.

"Apparently not everyone got that memo." The nurse had been more kind to Mara when he'd insisted she get checked out first. Then, when the tables had turned, Mara wouldn't stop fussing. It wasn't until she went upstairs that Billy realized the nurse wasn't going to cut him any slack. "So, what's going on?"

"Like I told you on the way over here, it's been confirmed that Bryan's stash isn't at the school," Matt started, taking a seat on the doctor's stool. He pulled out his pad to look at the notes he'd written. "After hearing what happened, Chief Hawser offered up a few of his off-duty officers to comb the school again, just in case. He said if that's stepping on your toes to let him know, but he didn't sound like he cared either way."

"I reckon he probably doesn't mind about stepping on anyone's toes," Billy said. "But that's not a bad idea."

"He also said his communications head suggests you hold a press conference to try and let the public know to look out for Beck, his associate and any suspicious activity." Matt cut him a grin. "I told him you already contacted the news station, right after you yelled at the EMTs to turn off the damn sirens because you couldn't hear yourself think."

Billy knew there was humor in what he'd done,

but when he'd woken in the ambulance on a stretcher, Mara peering down at him through her long, dark lashes, he'd been feeling anything but humorous. Part of him knew he needed to take it easy but the other part, the sheriff side of him, knew that time was wasting. Beck and his friend weren't going to take a break just because he needed one.

"Was Hawser the only chief in the county that called in so far?" Matt nodded. Billy bet Chief Calloway, from the city of Kipsy, would be on him soon. They were usually a bit busier than the rest of Riker, but Alexandria Calloway was not the kind of chief to sit back and twiddle her thumbs about any case.

Billy figured he might as well beat her to the punch. "I'll get Dane to talk to Chief Calloway and see if she can make sure all of her officers stay in the loop." His head thrummed with a dull ache. Like putting a shell up to his ear and hearing the ocean but, in Billy's case, he couldn't seem to put the shell down. The doctor had given him something for the pain and nausea but he'd refused to get the really good stuff. He had a job to do. He needed to stay sharp.

"While all of this posturing is going on, I need you to keep on trying to figure out who this Beck person is and who's helping him," Billy said. "Use Caleb as a start since he's the only person we actually know the identity of. Once I get out of here I'm going to call in a few reserve deputies to see if we can't narrow down a possibility as to where our friends are at least staying since we burned their hotel bridge."

Matt nodded. He wrote something down and

closed the pad. He looked a bit alarmed when Billy swung his legs over the bed and stood. Billy pointed at him.

"If you tell me to rest, I'll fire you on the spot," he threatened.

Matt's grin was back.

"Wouldn't dream of it."

"Good, now get to work. I'm going to go upstairs and then head back to the office."

It hadn't been until a little after he'd come to in the ambulance that Billy had learned Suzy had been shot. Luckily she'd been wearing her bulletproof vest beneath her uniform. The impact, however, had caused her to fall, shattering her radio and pushing her away from her cell phone. Robert, in terror, had started to run, and she'd had her hands full wrangling him back inside the gym. He had been so frenzied that he'd hyperventilated and passed out. Which no one blamed him for. He'd expected to simply show them around the school, maybe find something interesting in the process. Not almost get killed by an unknown shooter.

Suzy was standing in the hallway on the second floor in the east wing. She had a scowl on her face and her vest in her hand. Instead of her Riker County Sheriff's Department shirt, she was wearing a plain white T-shirt. When she saw Billy, her scowl deepened.

"He ruined my shirt," she greeted. "The bullet tore right through it."

"I'm sure we could order you a new one."

"Good."

Billy was next to her now and could tell she was holding back. But that's who Suzy was. She held her emotions close to her chest. Sometimes she didn't even let Billy in, and he was her closest friend.

"Besides the shirt, how's everything else?" he asked. Suzy brought her eyes up quick, her mouth stretching into a thin line. Defensive. Billy amended his question. "I mean with the vest. How's the vest doing?"

Suzy started to say something but paused. She let out a breath and played along.

"Okay," she admitted, face softening for a moment. "Glad it wasn't shot more than once, though. It's going to bruise something wicked."

Billy smiled.

"Won't we all."

Suzy nodded, gave her own little smirk and motioned to the room behind her. The door was shut but Billy knew who was behind it.

"How's Cassie doing?" He nodded to the room.

Suzy glanced over her shoulder.

"To be honest, I don't know. All I got is that she hasn't woken up since the surgery, but she's on some pretty intense meds so that's normal."

Billy tensed. For several reasons. One was that he hadn't seen Mara since she'd left him to go with Suzy to check on the trainee. Surely Suzy wouldn't just let her wander off.

"So, Mara's not in there?" he had to ask. It made Suzy's lip quirk up for a second. She pointed down to the other end of the hall.

"Don't worry, Sheriff. Your gal's right there."

Billy ignored the comment but was glad to see the dark-haired woman a few yards away. She stood talking to an older couple he recognized as Mr. and Mrs. Gates, Cassie's parents. He hadn't realized they had already flown in, probably relieving her sister who had a few kids at home. He'd meant to meet with them, but that intention had fallen through the cracks as their case had gone nowhere but south since Cassie had been hurt. Billy scrubbed his hand down his face and sighed. It sat heavy on his chest.

"Buck up, partner," Suzy whispered. "They're coming over."

"Mr. and Mrs. Gates, it's good to see you," Billy greeted them when they stopped. He had no doubt in that moment that neither would leave the hospital until their daughter did. "I'm just sorry it had to be under these circumstances."

Mrs. Gates, a woman who probably exercised her laugh lines during happier times, gave him a weak smile. She looked exhausted and withdrawn. A shadow of the woman Billy had met at Cassie's informal birthday gathering a handful of months before. Mr. Gates, who held the strain of his daughter's near-death experience clearly on his shoulders, was faster with a verbal greeting and a handshake.

"I'd have to agree with you there," he said, pumping Billy's hand once and letting it drop. His eyes dropped with it and focused on Suzy's vest. The chief deputy had tried to angle it behind her as they'd walked up, but Mr. Gates had a sharp eye. Or maybe he was just suspicious of anything and everything. Billy didn't blame him, considering. "The man who did that to Cassie shot you?" he asked Suzy.

"We can't say for certain," she responded. "But it's a possibility."

"Either way, both incidents are being investigated thoroughly by our entire department and other departments in the county," Billy assured him. "And we're about to go back out there and join them." The words didn't seem to offer Mrs. Gates any relief the way they did her husband. Mara must have sensed it. She lightly touched the woman's arm.

"These are good, smart people," she said. "Everyone responsible will be caught and dealt with. Don't you worry about that."

Mrs. Gates turned to look at Mara. She patted her hand and nodded.

"How's she doing, by the way?" Suzy asked. "We couldn't find the doctor, and the nurse just said she was sleeping."

This was a question Mrs. Gates was quicker to answer. There was a noticeable tremble in her voice as she did.

"She's good. The surgery was quick and they say everything will heal." She touched her neck. Her voice broke as she added, "She'll, uh—she'll have a scar, though."

"But a scar we'll take," Mr. Gates jumped in. He put his hands on his wife's arms and squeezed. The pressure seemed to jog her out of the worry she'd been falling back into.

She turned to him and smiled.

"You're right." She took one of his hands and they seemed to get lost in their own silent conversation. They loved each other. That much was apparent. It made Billy want to look at Mara.

He shouldn't have done what he'd done earlier. But being that close to Mara—touching her—he'd just wanted more. His body had taken hold over his mind and reached out for her again.

And she'd reached back.

"Well, you let us know if there's anything we can do for you, but it's time for us to get back out there," Billy said, eyes firm on the couple. He didn't need to look at Mara.

What had happened between them couldn't happen again. Not now.

"THEY GAVE ME something for the pain and wrapped me up," Mara said when she was riding shotgun in Billy's car. "Like I said, it's only a little bruising. No broken ribs. So I'm fine."

"I believe you."

His eyes flickered over to her but didn't settle. It made the guilt of everything that had happened rise again within her.

"Billy, I'm sorry," she said. "I thought the money and drugs would be at the school. I was wrong and you got hurt and Suzy got shot. I just—I'm so sorry."

"It's not your fault," he said with force. "It was a good lead. One we had to chase down, one way or the other." He slapped his hand on the steering wheel. It made Mara jump. "A lead *I* should have chased down. Not you. I shouldn't have dropped my guard." There appeared to be something else he wanted to say, but his original thought must have won out. "You got hurt, too."

Mara wanted to wave off his concern, but she realized he was right. In part. Her presence might have been the reason Beck and his lackey had shown up in the first place, thinking she knew where the stash was and following her to the school. If she'd stayed at Billy's, then the sheriff and his chief deputy wouldn't have had their lives put in danger. At least, no more than usual.

That line of thinking was a straight shot to Alexa. She was still at the Reed family home with Claire, unaware that she'd come close to losing her father.

"I'm sorry, Billy," Mara whispered before she even realized what she was saying. The haze of medication wasn't as thick as she wished it was. The kind of pain that couldn't be seen was coming to the forefront. The present danger they were in was just salt in her past choices' wounds. She wasn't talking about what had happened at the school anymore. "I know you must hate me."

Billy was silent a moment, probably piecing together a polite way to agree with her, when something she hadn't expected interrupted them.

A truck slammed into the side of their car, right behind Billy. It happened so fast that Mara didn't even have time to scream. The impact rocketed them off the road, past the shoulder and right into the ditch.

Wham-bam-bam!

It wasn't until they settled that Mara realized with relief that they hadn't flipped. She turned to look at Billy, ready to voice the thought, when she saw the sheriff's eyes were closed.

"Billy?" she heard herself screech.

When he opened his eyes, she would have jumped for joy if it wasn't for the seat belt that held her tight. He shook his head a little, dazed, and then seemed to snap out of it.

"You okay?" he asked, already moving.

"Yeah, I think so. What about who hit us?"

Billy whipped his head around and looked back out at the road. The Tahoe was turned at an angle that blocked whoever had hit them from Mara's view. So when Billy started cussing, she didn't understand. But then he said one name that put everything into terrifying perspective.

"Beck."

Chapter Fifteen

Mara's heartbeat was in her ears, thumping with unforgiving relentlessness. The spike in adrenaline wasn't helping. Nor Billy's warning for her to stay down.

And it sure didn't help matters that he'd pulled his gun out.

"Call Suzy" was all Billy said before he opened his door and took aim past the back end of the vehicle.

Mara undid her seat belt and tried to get as low as possible while fumbling for Billy's phone. She found it in a cup holder and dialed Suzy, trying to get her panic under control.

"Beck just hit us off the road," Mara rushed to explain as soon as the call connected. She followed with their location before Billy yelled.

"Come out with your hands up or I'll shoot," he warned. Mara couldn't hear if Beck answered.

"I'm a minute away," Suzy said. "Keep me on the line." Mara nodded to no one in particular and put the phone on speaker. She relayed the information to Billy.

"Having a shoot-out with the sheriff isn't a good idea," Billy hollered.

Mara wished she could see what was going on. Billy had half his body hanging out the open door and gun held high, but Mara couldn't believe it was good cover.

Would Beck really try to shoot him?

She didn't have to wonder for long.

A shot rang out. Mara gasped as the vehicle rocked.

"What happened?" Suzy yelled, but Billy had his own answer ready. He fired his gun once. It wasn't long before Beck returned fire, causing Billy to retaliate. Soon all Mara could hear was gunfire slamming into metal and glass. She couldn't tell who was hitting what. She kept her head covered and her body as low against the floorboards as she could, praying that Billy wasn't getting hit. When she saw the driver's side window spiderweb from a bullet, mere inches from Billy, Mara nearly cried.

However, when the back windshield shattered, covering the interior in a hail of glass, Mara couldn't help but scream. She closed her eyes tight and covered her head. Around the pounding of her own heart, she expected to hear the shots even more clearly without the back window, but then everything went silent.

"What's going on?" she whispered to Billy.

The sheriff's posture was rigid—a stance that said there was no way in hell he was moving until this was over—but he answered her after a moment.

"Beck got back into the car," he said. "The windows are tinted. I can't see either one of them now."

So Beck had his friend with him.

Maybe because that left him more vulnerable than he liked, Billy got back into the driver's seat and shut his door. His head stayed turned, keeping an eye on the truck. It was still on the road, level with them, but at an angle that gave neither Billy nor Beck a good, clean shot.

"They're leaving," Billy yelled, angry.

"Let's go after them!" Mara might not have liked the danger but, with a surge of anger herself, she knew then that the men weren't going to stop.

So *they* needed to be stopped.

"They shot out a tire. I tried to do the same but my angle was off," he growled. "Suzy, they're moving down Meadows, southbound. Driving the same truck Mara described when she came to town. They're missing some windows."

Suzy confirmed she heard while Billy got his radio. He gave an order for the deputies in the area to help Suzy. He also told dispatch to send a tow truck. She asked if they needed medical attention. It seemed to snap Billy out of sheriff mode. His eyes softened with concern. So much of it that Mara felt the sudden urge to wrap herself around him. To comfort him. To feel comfort from him. To feel him.

"I'm okay," she assured him instead. "Are you?"

Billy nodded, but Mara still traced every inch of him she could with her eyes. He told dispatch to hold off on the medic. When he was done with his orders, Billy scrubbed a hand down his face. A sigh as heavy as a boulder seemed to crush him.

"I agree with that sigh," Mara said, moving slowly, gingerly, back to a sitting position. She couldn't help but wince, pain meds or not. Billy's hand covered hers.

Expecting his eyes to be as soft as they had been moments before, Mara was surprised again by the man. He looked like he was ready to kill.

"We have to end this," he said, voice hard as stone. Mara was about to agree, but then the sheriff said something that stopped her cold. "Mara, we have to talk to your father."

THE DRIVE OUT to Walter Correctional Facility took them an hour out of Riker County. In that hour, Mara had barely spoken a word. As he sat across from her father now, Billy didn't blame her one bit for needing the silence to collect her thoughts. She might have to face a man not even Billy wanted to deal with. But the fact of the matter was that Beck was escalating. Ambushing them at the school and then less than a few hours later attacking them again, this time on a well-traveled public road?

It all reeked of desperation.

Billy believed that if Mara hadn't screamed, probably making Beck and his associate remember they needed her alive, that the outcome would have been different. But she had and they'd sped off, disappearing before Suzy or any deputies could catch up to them.

Now here Billy was. In an interview room within

the prison looking at a man he'd wished to never see again.

Bryan Copeland had been balding for years but he had never let a thing like losing his hair conflict with his image. He was a confident man. Always had been. He'd always worn suits and expensive cologne, and had a quick wit about him that made people laugh. He was a people person, a schmoozer, a go-get-them type filled with determination and steeped in self-esteem.

Bryan Copeland had been kind and cunning in his dealings with the general public and one hell of a dancer at parties. To his underlings, however, he had been cutthroat. Like night and day, when Bryan needed to get down to business he stripped off his disguise and showed his true face. His wit became a weapon, his charm a tool. Whatever compassion he exuded in his home life and within the community was replaced with menace and greed.

That was the man Billy sat in front of now.

Dressed in prison orange, Bryan Copeland looked across the table at him with the eyes of a snake ready to strike.

"Well merry Christmas to me," he greeted Billy. "Couldn't stay away from the man who made your career possible, *Sheriff*?"

Billy had nothing to prove to the man. Nothing to defend, either. At the time, Billy hadn't known stopping Bryan would help him become sheriff. He'd just wanted to stop the man and his business before both destroyed his home.

A choice he didn't regret and never would.

"I have some questions for you."

Bryan scoffed.

"If you can't do your job, *Sheriff*, then I'm certainly not going to do it for you."

Billy ignored his comment and put the sketch of Beck on the table between them. He kept it turned over. Bryan's eyes never strayed to it.

"Where's your secret stash?"

Bryan didn't flinch.

"First of all, that's a ridiculous question that makes you sound like you're some preteen on a treasure hunt," Bryan said. "Secondly, I don't have a secret stash."

"And third?" Billy asked with a low sigh. Bryan's nostrils flared. He didn't like it when the person he was talking to showed disinterest or contempt. It rubbed against his ego, something he'd been fluffing for decades.

"If I did have a secret stash, of whatever it is you think I have, why in hell would I ever tell you about it?" Bryan was nearly seething. His dislike for Billy was pure. The moment he'd found out that Mara had betrayed him and helped Billy was the moment Bryan Copeland began to hate him more than anyone in the world.

That's how Billy knew that just asking would get him nowhere.

So, he was going to gun for the man's precious pride instead.

"Because, if you don't tell me where it is, this man will eventually find it." Billy flipped over the picture and pushed it toward him. "And he'll use it to pick up where you left off. But this time he'll do it better, smarter and with your help whether you want to give it or not. He'll take your legacy and make it his own. In fact, he's already started."

Bryan's lips had thinned but his expression remained blank. His eyes, however, trailed down to the picture. If he recognized Beck, it didn't register in his face or posture. When he answered, he seemed as uptight as he had been when he'd been escorted into the room.

"I don't know what you came here to try and accomplish, but I can tell you now that you should have saved the gas." Bryan fingered the picture. "I don't know this man and I don't know his business. What I *do* know is that if I had a *secret stash* it would have been found during the investigation. Unless you're admitting to me now that you're not that great at your job. Which, again, to be honest, I already knew." Bryan's eyes turned to slits. His nostrils flared. "Why else would you need my daughter's help to catch me?"

Billy knew in that moment that the only way he'd get an answer was to use Mara. Because Bryan Copeland might appear to be a man who wasn't affected by the world, but the truth was he had one weakness.

His daughter.

He'd loved her so much that he hadn't ever entertained the idea that she could turn on him. That she *would* turn on him. That's why he was handcuffed to a table, sitting in an interrogation room with an armed guard behind him.

But Billy wanted to keep her out of the room for as long as he could. So he leveled with her father.

"This man goes by the name Beck," Billy started. "As far as we know, he has one associate who isn't afraid of killing. One or both of them were involved in the murders of three people, two of whom were in police custody when they were killed. They are also responsible for putting three people in the hospital, but that wasn't because of mercy. It's because the people they hurt got lucky." Billy purposely didn't name anyone who had been killed or attacked. He knew Bryan wouldn't care. His response confirmed that belief.

"So? I've had nothing to do with this Beck person or his friend. And if you don't believe me then I'm sure the warden won't mind giving me an alibi." He motioned to the room around them, as if Billy needed the fact that he was in prison emphasized.

"I'm telling you because the only reason we know about Beck is because he showed up at your daughter's house and threatened her." An almost imperceptible shift occurred in the man across from him. Billy didn't know if Bryan did or did not know Beck but the fact that the man had been to see his daughter was news to him. "Since then he's had people try to kidnap her, put her in the hospital and they've even shot at her. All because they think she knows where this stash of yours is located."

Bryan laughed out loud. This time Billy was the one who was surprised.

"They think she might be in cahoots with her old

man, huh?" he said around another bite of laughter. It wasn't the kind filled with mirth or humor. It was dark. Menacing. "You and I both know how wrong the assumption that my daughter and I work together is, don't we, *Sheriff*?" He lowered his voice. Despite the decrease in volume, his words thundered. "The one who would rather be in your bed than a part of my life."

Billy was trying not to let Bryan get to him, but that one comment created an almost feral reaction within him. One where he felt the need to protect Mara's name and, to some degree, protect himself.

It bothered Billy the way Mara's only family talked about her with such distaste—such hate—while he also had never liked the fact that Bryan suspected he and Mara had been together. It wasn't that Billy had been ashamed of her—he hadn't ever been—but they'd told only a few people about their relationship. Bryan had not only guessed but been certain that Billy and Mara were together. Which meant Bryan Copeland was either really good at reading his daughter or Billy…or someone had told him.

Regardless of which it was, Billy was still bothered by it. He stood and went to the guard next to the door.

"Bring her in," he said, low enough that Bryan couldn't hear.

The guard nodded and left.

Billy returned to the table but didn't sit down. Instead, he moved to the corner of the room.

"And what tactic is this?" Bryan asked, amused. "Trying to intimidate me by sending the guard away?

There are much more intimidating men in this place, Sheriff. With some tricks that end in death. This isn't going to—"

The door started to open.

"This isn't a trick," Billy interrupted. He nodded in the direction of the guard. Mara was behind him. Her back was straight, her shoulders straight, and her eyes sharp and cautious. She rounded the table and took a seat across from her father.

The amusement Bryan had shown Billy disappeared in an instant. If it was possible, he seemed to sit up straighter, as if a board had been attached to his back. With the two of them mirroring each other, Billy realized how much the father and daughter looked alike.

Mara was the first to speak.

"Hey, Dad."

Chapter Sixteen

"You've got more nerve coming here than he does."

Mara wasn't surprised by her father's response, but that didn't mean it didn't still hurt a little. She kept her face as expressionless as she could and tried to remember why they were there. Why she was subjecting herself to the emotional torture she'd tried to avoid for two years.

For Alexa, she thought. *To stop this madness once and for all.*

"I'm tired of being hunted, Dad," she said. "Beck—"

Bryan slammed his fist against the tabletop. Mara jumped.

"You wouldn't be hunted if you hadn't betrayed me," he snarled. "You made your bed when you turned on the only family you had and *both* of you are just going to have to lie in it!"

Billy started to move forward, already trying to defend her, Mara was sure, but she hadn't had her say yet.

"You tried to create a drug empire out of an entire

county, Dad. That's three towns and a city worth of people," she responded. "What was I supposed to do when I found out? Sit back and watch?"

"You should have come to me," he seethed. "Not him. I'm your *father*, your flesh and blood. I raised you, kept food on the table and a roof over your head. I bent over backwards to make sure you never wanted for anything. And now, what do I get in return? A prison cell, Mara! A damn prison cell!"

This time Mara heard Billy begin to speak but she'd had enough.

"Do you remember what you told me when you decided to move to Kipsy? You said you moved because you needed a slower pace. That you wanted to relax. Those were *your* words. And then you asked me to move there, too. Do you remember what I told you?" Mara was yelling now. Whatever dam was holding her emotions back had broken the moment her father spoke. When he didn't answer, it was Mara's turn to slam her hand against the table. It hurt but she ignored the pain.

"I said I didn't want to," she continued. "I had a good life that I didn't want to leave. I had a good job, friends and a home. But no. When I came down to visit, you talked about missing me and being lonely and how Kipsy was a good city filled with good people. You painted this picture of a life you knew I'd always wanted. One where we'd be happy, where I'd meet a good man, raise a family, and you'd sit on your front porch swinging with your grandkids and sipping sweet tea. I could even start a business and have the dream job I'd always wished for. You tried so hard to convince me to love the idea of Kipsy that it worked. I fell in love with it. So, what did you expect would happen when you started to destroy it all?"

"You could have still had all of those things," he responded, more quietly than he had been before. "I always protected you. You were never in any danger. You could have had everything, but, instead, you sided with *him*."

Her father's eyes cut to Billy with such a look of disgust in them that the dam within her disintegrated further until there was nothing left. Mara fisted her hands and, for the first time in years, yelled at her father so loudly she felt her face heat.

"Don't you *dare* blame Billy or me or *anyone* else for your mistakes. You made them and now you're the one who has to take responsibility for them!" Mara took out the picture she'd tucked into her back pocket. She hadn't planned on using it, but she'd recognized the possibility that she might have to. She slammed the picture down and slid it over to him, next to the picture of Beck.

"You may hate me, Dad. You may not care what Beck and his friends will do to me. You may even want something bad to happen to me. But what about her?" Just seeing the smiling face of Alexa looking up from the picture calmed Mara. Her voice lowered to an even level but she didn't drop any of the hostility. Her father's eyes stayed on the picture as she continued. "This is your granddaughter, Alexa. She didn't investigate you and she certainly didn't have a hand in putting you in here. So, *please*, *Dad*, don't make her pay for our mistakes."

Mara was done. There was nothing left for her to say—to add—to try and sway her father to tell them if he really had a stash and, if so, where it was. She was exhausted. Drained. Yet relieved in a way, too. Not only was she facing her father but she had said exactly what she'd always wanted to.

His eyes stayed on the picture but he didn't say anything right away. Billy took advantage of the silence, perhaps sensing Mara was out of ideas.

"These men believe without a doubt that you have a stash and Mara knows exactly where it is. They've also made it clear that they don't care what happens to Alexa in the process of trying to find it or use Mara. They'll kill her, and then eventually they'll kill your daughter." Even as he said it, she knew he hated the words. Mara knew the feeling. Just the mention of harm to Alexa had a knot forming in her stomach.

"There's no wedding ring on your finger," her father said after a moment. "But she's his, isn't she?" His eyes were slits of rage as he looked at Billy, but she knew what he said next was aimed at her. "Don't you dare lie to me about this."

"We're not together, but yes, she's mine," Billy answered.

The simple admission that Billy was, indeed, Alexa's father should have made Mara happy, and it did—but the first part of the sentence hurt more than she expected. She strained to keep her expression as blank as possible. Maybe the last few days had just been two people caught up in madness, trying to comfort each other for different reasons. Maybe, when everything was said and done, they'd go back to their lives with the only link between them being Alexa. Maybe it had been lust and not love that had tangled them together.

Her father was watching her intently. She didn't need to think about the future when the present was being threatened.

"You two come up here like I owe you something I don't," Bryan Copeland said, standing. "Using a granddaughter I didn't even know existed isn't the way to get me to tell you anything. I can't help you." He turned and looked to the guard. "I'm done talking with them."

"Bryan," Billy tried, but the man wasn't having any of it. Before he was escorted from the room, he looked at Billy. There was nothing but sincerity when he spoke.

"Watch out for daughters, Sheriff. They'll stab you in the back every time."

"Reed, hold up a second."

Billy paused in his walk to the car. Mara, however, didn't. She hadn't said a word since Bryan left. Her eyes, dark and deep, had stayed dead ahead as they went through the process of leaving the prison.

The guard who'd been in the room with the three of them, a man named Ned, jogged up to Billy, mouth already open and ready to talk. Billy wondered if he'd forgotten some procedure for signing out. If so, he hoped it wouldn't take too long. The day had turned into a scorcher.

"I know it was none of my business to listen but sometimes you can't help it when you're in the room." Ned shrugged. "But I didn't know if you caught on to what Mr. Copeland was talking about when he said he wouldn't tell you anything."

Billy felt his eyebrow rise.

"And you do?"

"I guess I can't speak with complete certainty in Mr. Copeland's case, but you see, there's a different kind of world here," he said, thrusting his thumb over his shoulder to the prison. "There are men serving time in there who have done a hell of a lot worse than run drugs. Men who take to killing like it was nothing. Heck, some of them don't even break a sweat trying to do the same thing even when they're living in a cell."

"Yeah, I'd imagine that's true. But what's that have to do with anything?" Billy was frustrated. Not at the man in front of him, but in general. He didn't want to stand out in the heat and talk about prison politics if he could help it.

"What I'm saying is that a man like Bryan Copeland may look intimidating to the general public with his tidiness and fancy talk, but in there—" again he thrust his thumb back over his shoulder "—in there he doesn't have anything going for him. But he's never had any problems as far as we know."

Billy was about to tell the man to go back inside if he wasn't going to be helpful, but then he heard Bryan's words again.

"He said, *I can't help you* not *I won't*," Billy realized. Ned nodded.

"My guess, if that money or whatever exists, he's using it as insurance to keep him safe in here." Ned shrugged. "I could be way off, but it's happened before."

"So keeping the stash hidden might be the only thing keeping him alive in there."

Ned nodded. "He could use it to buy protection from certain inmates or use it as leverage," Ned confirmed.

"Any idea who he might be targeted by if someone was trying to kill him?"

Ned's expression hardened. The new tension in his shoulders let Billy know he'd not be getting an answer from the guard.

"I don't know," he supplied. "Sorry."

"No problem," Billy said. "At least we have an idea of why he won't tell us." Billy cast a look at Mara. She was leaning against the car, looking out at the road in the distance. Even from where he stood, Billy knew she wasn't there with them. Her thoughts had carried her miles and miles away. "But knowing that might not be a good thing."

"Why's that?" the guard asked.

"Because it still means that Bryan would rather protect himself than protect his daughter and granddaughter."

MARA DIDN'T SAY anything for the majority of their drive back, much like the drive there. But this time, she wasn't sure if it was for the same reasons.

She kept her gaze out the windshield, watching as the road disappeared beneath them. Billy had told her what Ned the guard had said, but that was only the cherry on top of a trip she shouldn't have taken. Any relief she'd felt at finally confronting her dad, telling him about his granddaughter and admitting Billy was the father was no longer warming off the cold that had been sitting like a rock in her stomach.

Not only was her father not going to help them, he'd made it very clear that she was no longer wanted in his life. Which, to be honest, she had expected— yet there she was, feeling the sting of it still.

Mara leaned her head back against the headrest and closed her eyes.

The emotional strain of seeing her father—and the past that she'd never be able to change, even if she wanted to—had wiped Mara out physically.

However, no sooner had her eyes closed than Mara was back in that room with Billy saying they weren't together. It shouldn't have bothered her, considering it was a fact she already knew, but still… The finality of the words, said in the strong, clear voice she'd come to enjoy more than she should have, had broken something within her. In a way that she hadn't expected.

Mara let out what she thought was a quiet sigh. One that let the outside world know she was having an internal battle.

"We need to talk about everything that happened."

She opened one eye and looked over at the sheriff. He was frowning something fierce. Mara closed her eye again.

"I don't want to," she admitted. "Not right now, at least."

"But, Mara—"

"Billy, please, don't," she interrupted. "There's only so much a person can deal with all at once. I just want to get back and see my daughter. Okay?"

The Bronco lurched to the side. Mara's eyes flashed open to see Billy cutting the wheel. They'd made it into Riker County according to a sign they'd passed a few miles back, but that didn't mean Mara recognized the Presbyterian church or the parking lot they now were turning into.

"What are you doing?" Mara asked, anger coming to the forefront of her question. It was misplaced, she knew, but that didn't stop it from turning her cheeks hot or spiking her adrenaline enough to make her sit up straight.

"We're going to talk," Billy said, parking in a row of cars already in the lot. A few people were meandering near the entrance to the church but didn't seem interested in them.

"What do you mean we're going to talk? Isn't that what we've been doing?"

Billy put the car in Park, took off his seat belt and turned his body enough that he was facing her straight on. His mouth was set in a frown and yet, somehow, it still begged to be touched.

To be kissed.

Mara shook her head, trying to clear the thought, as Billy confronted her.

"You're shutting down," he said, serious. His eyes

had changed their shade of green from forest to that of tall ferns bowing in a breeze.

"I don't even know what that means," she said, keeping her eyes firmly on his gaze.

Billy's expression didn't soften. He wasn't interested in playing nice anymore. Before he said a word, Mara knew where the conversation would eventually lead.

"What you just went through can't have been easy and now you don't want to talk about it? Even with me?"

"Even with you?" The last shred of emotional sanity Mara had started to fray. "You know everything I do about this case. You heard everything my father said in there. Beyond that, there's nothing you have to do to help me. It isn't your job to make sure I talk about my feelings. We aren't together, Billy. Not anymore."

For whatever reason, using Billy's words from earlier against him made Mara break further. She unbuckled her seat belt and fumbled for the door handle. Tears began to blur her vision.

"I-I need a moment," she said before Billy could get a word in edgewise. Mara opened the door and walked out into the heat.

And swiftly away from the Riker County sheriff.

Chapter Seventeen

Mara had to think. She had to walk. She had to move so the pain of everything wouldn't settle. Her father's words, Billy's words, Beck's words all rattled around in her mind. Taunting her, comforting her, threatening her. Why couldn't life have stayed simple? Why had her father turned out the way he had? Why had she fallen in love with the one man Riker County needed to protect it?

Mara made it out of the parking lot and to a small park beside the church before she heard footsteps behind her. She'd spent the short walk trying desperately not to cry. The strain already was pushing in a headache.

Sure, it made sense to be upset about everything. Her father *had* just chosen himself over her and her child. But what bothered her the most was that, at the moment, all she could do was think about Billy.

"Mara, stop."

A hand closed around her arm and gently held her still. Mara blinked several times to try and dissuade any tears from falling. Instead of turning her around, Billy stepped into view.

Mara felt the sudden urge to take his hat off and put her hand through his hair.

It all hurt even more, knowing with absolute certainty that she'd never stop wanting Billy Reed.

"Talk to me," he prodded. He lowered his head to look into her eyes more easily.

"Why haven't you asked me?" Mara blurted before she could police her thoughts. "Why haven't you asked one single question about why I left or why I didn't tell you about Alexa?" Billy dropped his hand from her arm. A piece of her heart fell with it. "Just ask me, Billy. At least one question. Please."

Tears threatened to spill again, but Mara stilled herself, waiting for an answer. This time, they weren't interrupted and Billy asked a question Mara hadn't expected.

"Would you have ever told me about her?"

Mara realized then that there would never have been a good time to talk about the choices she'd made. That, at the end of the day, she'd kept one heck of a secret. One that would hurt someone, no matter what. Billy's expression was open and clear as a bell, but she knew his tone well enough to realize it was a man waiting for bad news.

She had already hurt him with her silence. It was time to tell him the truth.

All of it.

"You may not believe me now, and I don't blame you for that, but I never meant to keep her a secret in the first place," Mara started. A breeze swept through the park. She wrapped her arms around herself, even though she wasn't cold. "I found out I was pregnant with her two days before you became sheriff. You remember how quiet I was then? You kept asking me if I was okay."

She watched as Billy slipped back into his own memories.

"I thought it was because of your dad," he admitted. "He'd just gotten sentenced." Mara gave him a sympathetic smile. His eyes widened. "Why didn't you tell me then?"

"I planned to, at dinner that night," she said. "I wanted everything to be nice… But I forgot to get eggs for the cake."

Billy's eyebrow rose in question. Why did that matter? he was most likely wondering.

"Do you remember Donna Ramsey? The woman we saw at the coffee shop?" Billy nodded. "Well, I went back out to buy eggs and ran into her. She wasn't happy at seeing me." Mara remembered the look of absolute hatred burning in the woman's eyes. It wasn't a look she'd ever forget. "Do you know that her husband died overseas? And that her daughter was all the family she had left in the world?" Mara didn't wait for Billy to answer. "Kennedy Ramsey killed herself when her girlfriend overdosed on Moxy. Donna was the one who found her." Mara felt her face harden. Her vision started to blur with the tears she couldn't stop. Caught between anger and sadness, she couldn't tell which emotion had its claws in her heart at the moment.

"I didn't know that," Billy admitted. "But around then it was hard to see all of the repercussions."

"Well, Donna's hatred for me is one that I saw up close."

"It wasn't your fault what happened," Billy asserted.

"If I had come to you earlier about my father—" she started.

"It could have taken us just as long to figure out how to trap him," he jumped in. "Despite our intentions, your father was a very clever man. Two weeks might not have made any difference at all."

Mara shrugged.

"Either way, Donna let me know I was just as much to blame as my father was," Mara continued. "She told me that she would never accept me in Carpenter or Kipsy and neither would anyone else. To prove her point, the cashier who had overheard the exchange refused to check me out." Mara tried a small smile. "That's why there was no cake at dinner."

"But—"

"I didn't want to tell you that night because all I could think about was Donna, all alone, cursing my family's name," Mara explained, cutting him off. "And so I decided I'd tell you the next day, but then you spent it with Sheriff Rockwell and were so excited that, once again, I decided to wait. I wanted you to celebrate to your heart's content. You'd waited so long for the opportunity to be sheriff."

Mara was getting to the part that she'd once thought she'd never tell Billy. But, standing together now, Mara finally felt like she could tell him everything. She didn't want anything left unsaid. She wanted a clean slate again.

She *needed* it.

"I was going to tell you after the ceremony because I couldn't keep it in anymore. I was scared but excited," she continued. The dull throb in her side started to gnaw at her, as if opening up emotional wounds was somehow affecting her physical ones. "I was at the ceremony, standing in the crowd, off to the side, where I hoped no one would notice me. But then someone did. He asked me if I was proud of you— and I was, Billy. I was so proud of you. And he used that against me. He told me that as long as we were together, everything you had worked for would fall apart when people found out about us. The daughter of a man who nearly destroyed the county with the new sheriff sworn to protect it. Billy, I looked up at you and you were so happy, and I couldn't get Donna out of my head and—" Mara couldn't help it. A sob tore from her lips and she began to cry. Overcome with emotions long since buried, she finally got to the heart of the matter. "And, Billy, I believed him. If I stayed, I was sure people would hate you because of me, and I just couldn't take that. I'd rather live with the guilt of being Bryan Copeland's daughter than knowing I was the reason you lost your home."

Billy remained quiet for a moment. His expression was unreadable. Even to her. Every part of Mara felt exposed, raw. Leaving Billy Reed had been the hardest thing she'd ever done.

She waited, trying to rein in her tears. Then, like a switch had been flipped, Billy smiled.

"But Mara, you're forgetting something," he said, closing the space between them. He put his hands on either side of her face, holding every ounce of her attention within his gaze. Every hope she had of the future, every regret she had from the past. All at the mercy of the dark-haired sheriff.

"What?" she whispered, tears sliding down her cheeks. Billy brushed one away with his thumb, his skin leaving a trail of warmth across her cheek.

"*You* are my home."

Then Billy kissed her full on the lips.

Finally, Mara Copeland felt peace.

Unlike their shared moment earlier in the day, this kiss was slower. Deeper. It seemed to extend past her lips and dip into her very core. If he hadn't been holding her, Mara was sure she would have fallen. The kiss was affecting every part of her body, not excluding her knees. They trembled with relief and pleasure and promise as the kiss kept going.

If they had been anywhere other than a public park, it might have gone even further, but reality broke through the fantasy quickly. Billy pulled away, lips red, eyes hooded and with a question already poised.

"Wait, who talked to you at the ceremony?" Billy asked. "I respected your wishes for us to be a secret until things settled down. I only told the people who needed to know and I trusted all of them. They wouldn't have told," he added, sure in his words.

Mara let out a small sigh. She didn't want to create any bad blood between the sheriff and one of his deputies. Marsden had only told her his opinion. She had been the one who had listened to it.

"Deputy Marsden," she confessed. Billy's body instantly tensed. Mara rushed to defuse his anger. "He seemed really concerned. I think he was just looking out for you. You can't get mad at someone for loyalty."

Billy didn't appear to be listening to her. His eyes were locked with hers, but he wasn't seeing her.

"What is it?" Mara grabbed his hand. She squeezed it. "Billy?" The contact shook him out of his head. He didn't look like he'd be smiling any time soon.

"Marsden held no loyalty or fondness for me," he growled. "The last order of business Sheriff Rockwell attended to before I stepped in was letting Marsden go. That was one of the reasons Rockwell wanted to talk before the ceremony. If he found out about us, it was by accident. I never would have told him. Gene Marsden is not a good man, and the last I talked to him, he cursed my name."

"What?" Mara asked, surprised. She didn't remember hearing about Marsden being fired. Then again, it wasn't like she had stuck around to get the news, either.

"I'd completely forgotten about him. He was with us when we arrested Bryan. He must have heard your father when *he* was cursing my name about being with you. He—"

They both heard the noise too late, both wrapped up in their conversation.

"Sorry to interrupt."

All Mara had time to do was watch Billy tense.

Beck had the element of surprise and he used it swiftly. He pointed the shotgun right at Billy's chest.

"We'll just call this take three for the day."

BILLY WAS LOOKING at the wrong end of the barrel of a shotgun. Holding it was Beck, smiling ear to ear. Billy noticed a cut across the man's cheek, and he took some small satisfaction that he'd probably caused it not more than four hours ago.

"Hey there, Sheriff," Beck said, voice calm. "How you doing this fine day?"

When Billy had turned, he'd put Mara behind him. Even though she was out of the line of fire, that didn't mean he felt good about their situation. Especially since Beck was holding a shotgun. It would be hard to shield Mara from a shell blast from only a few feet away.

"Hadn't figured I'd see you again any time soon. I thought after shooting up your truck you'd be long gone," Billy admitted. "Where is your friend? I'd like to repay him for the knock on the head he gave me." He glanced over Beck's shoulder to see if anyone at the church had noticed that there was a man holding a gun on them. But no one seemed to be any the wiser.

"Oh, look at you, always the dutiful sheriff. In a bad situation and still trying to fish for information." Even though there was humor in his tone, Beck's hold on the gun was serious. Billy's own gun was burning in its holster. They never should have left the car. He never should have pulled over. Not when none of the deputies had found even a trace of the truck. But, when Mara was involved, Billy's actions didn't always make sense. He cursed himself. He'd let his guard down again. There was no excuse for that. "Well, I'm sorry to disappoint you. I'm not here to answer your questions or theories or even suspicions. I have work to do."

"You're not as clever as you think," Mara said at Billy's shoulder. He was proud that her voice was even.

That's my girl.

Beck's smile turned to a smirk, a transformation that gave away the pleasure he must be feeling holding a gun on them. So far he'd shown he didn't believe in an even playing field. Why should now be any different? He was just going to have to find out the hard way that Billy was the kind of man who would go down fighting, especially when there was someone to fight for.

"You don't think I'm clever enough?" Beck asked. "Because I've been so bad at following you, hurting you and pulling guns on you? Or am I not that clever because I haven't killed you two yet?"

Billy's muscles tingled in anticipation.

If he could close the gap between him and the end of the shotgun, he might be able to grab it and move it enough that Mara could run for the car. If he was faster than the shot, that was. If he could disarm Beck or manage to get his own gun out, he could end this. Once and for all.

"Sheriff, calm down," Beck chided. "I'm not going to kill you or Miss Copeland right now. Maybe down the line, if it becomes an issue, but not right now."

"Then put down the gun," Billy ground out. It made Beck laugh.

"Don't mistake mercy for being an idiot. I still have a job to do right now. I didn't just follow you to have a little chat, now, did I?"

"What do you want, then?" Mara asked.

"Funny you should ask, Miss Copeland. Considering it's you."

"I don't think so," Billy cut in. "You're not taking her."

"Oh, but Sheriff, I am. And, what's more, you're going to let me."

Chapter Eighteen

Billy didn't like the confidence the man in front of him was exuding. There was no shaking of his hands as he held the gun, no quiver or tremble or even a fluctuation in his voice. Standing outside, in a public place, holding a gun on a sheriff and a civilian, Beck should have been showing some signs of anxiety or nervousness.

When, in reality, he was showing none.

Which meant one of two things. He was either stupid or he had one hell of an ace up his sleeve.

"And how do you figure that?" Billy asked. "Because I'm here to tell you, that's a tall order you're placing."

"It's because I know your secret," Beck said, simply. "And I intend to use that to make you two do exactly as I please."

Billy didn't need to see Mara to know she reacted in some way to Beck's threat. He himself had tensed, despite trying to appear impassive.

"Secret?" He didn't want to play into Beck's game but, at the same time, he didn't really have a choice.

"If I hadn't already known you two were an item, I would have guessed by that kiss just now," Beck pointed out. "You two really are terrible at hiding this *thing*." He nodded to them when he said *thing*.

"So?" Mara said. "We kissed. How are you going to make me leave willingly with that?"

"I can't." Beck shrugged. "But luckily that's not the only secret you two share. In fact, right now my associate is looking at that other secret of yours. She's pretty cute, you know."

Beck shifted his gaze to Billy with a level of nonchalance he didn't like. Pure rage and fear exploded within Billy's chest. It must have extended to Mara. He felt her hand on his back. A light touch, but with a heaviness only a worrying parent could carry. Beck tilted his head a little, as if waiting for them to fall over themselves responding. His impatience got the better of him. He exhaled, all dramatic.

"Do I need to spell it out for you, Sheriff?" he added.

Billy wasn't ready to believe the man had any kind of connection to his daughter. He could be bluffing for all Billy knew.

"Yes, you do," Billy answered. "We don't want to play any more games with you."

Beck's smile twitched, his nostrils flared and then he was all smirk again. His eyes went over Billy's shoulder to the park behind them. It remained focused on something—or someone—but Billy wasn't going to turn his back to the man.

"I guess you're right," Beck agreed. "Who has time

for stupid little games. Here's the deal—the bottom line. I'm short staffed, thanks to the two of you, I'm impatient and I'm over being out in this damn heat. Mara's going to tell me where that stash is and then I'm going to keep her until I've moved it. Then I'll let her go. You may be asking why should you trust me on that? Well." Beck's sneer fell into the most serious expression Billy had ever seen on the man. "Considering you two seem to be an item, how smart would I be if I killed the lover of the beloved sheriff? You'd never stop hunting me until it consumed you or you caught me. Those are odds I don't like playing. Am I wrong?"

Billy shook his head. "No. You aren't."

Mara moved her thumb on his back, a few strokes to show affection or appreciation. Either way, it eased a part of Billy. If only a little.

"Only a fool, or someone out of options, would make that mistake. I don't fall into either category," Beck assured them. "Also only a fool would directly kill the sheriff if it could be avoided, because then that's just painting a target on my head." Beck shook the shotgun a little, not taking it off them but reminding them he still had it. And that they were still in its sights. "But don't misunderstand that as me saying I won't shoot you. I will. But how could you help Alexa and Mara then, Billy?"

The hand on Billy's back dropped. Mara stepped from behind him and stopped at his side. Her expression was blank, but he knew she was filled with a cocktail of emotions, ready to spill out if she was pushed too hard.

"The bottom line," Billy said, words dripping with absolute disgust.

"Mara is going to come with me now and you're going to let her, or you'll never see your daughter again."

"You son of a—" Billy started, but Mara cut him off.

"What have you done?" she asked. Her voice was so calm, so even, it made Billy pause in his rant. It was the steady ice of a mother calculating a situation.

"Nothing. Yet. And it'll stay that way if you come with me." This time Beck's attention was on Mara.

"Alexa is safe," Billy cut in. "You're bluffing."

"And what if she isn't? What if I'm not bluffing?" Beck asked. "Are you going to take that chance, Sheriff?" He returned his attention to Mara. "And are you going to let him take that chance?"

"Mara—" Billy started.

"I want proof," she interrupted. "Or I won't go."

Beck let out a small exhale, frustrated. But he at least was accommodating. Even if it wasn't at all what Billy wanted to hear.

"Billy's mother, Claire, put up more of a fight than Deputy Mills did," Beck started. Every part of Billy contracted. A cold fire spread through him. Anger and fear warred with each other inside him. If that shotgun hadn't been between them, Billy could have ripped the man apart with his bare hands. "In his defense, he never saw my guy coming. But Claire was looking out the kitchen window, so by the time my associate went inside she'd already grabbed a gun and tried to hide the girl. Luckily for both of us, Claire's a bad shot and my guy has a code about killing the elderly, something to do with being raised by his grandmother, I suppose." Mara's hand went to her mouth. Billy fisted his hand so hard he'd bet he was drawing blood. Beck went on as though he was recapping a soap opera episode and not sharing one of the most terrifying situations a parent could hear. "Alexa was in the corner of a closet, a blanket thrown over her head. She was crying so hard that my associate grabbed her bag of toys. I haven't heard yet if they've worked on calming her down."

"You bastard," Billy snarled. His heartbeat was racing now, adrenaline mixing up everything he was already feeling.

"She's just a baby," Mara added. Her voice shook.

"And I'm just a businessman," Beck added. "An impatient one. If you don't come with me now, so help me, I will throw out what little morals I have left and make you two regret ever trying to get in my way."

Billy's stomach bottomed out. He glanced at Mara. She was looking at him. Her dark eyes were glassed over and wide, searching for some way to save Alexa. To save him. Because he knew she'd do anything to keep everyone safe. Just like Billy knew right then that Beck had won. Mara would go with him. And Billy would let her.

Beck's attention swiveled over his shoulder again. This time it was followed by a woman gasping.

"Hey, come here slowly or I'll shoot you," Beck yelled. Billy turned to see an older woman standing a few feet behind them. She must not have noticed there had been a shotgun in their discussion until she was closer. Her terrified eyes took the three of them in. "Come here now," Beck demanded. It was a few shades darker than any tone he'd used with Billy and Mara. It was made to intimidate quickly.

And it worked.

The woman walked over to them. Billy hoped she didn't have a heart attack.

"Now, what's your name?"

"Sa-Sally."

"Hey, Sally. My friend here needs his gun taken away," Beck said with a nod to Billy. "And I need you to do it for me."

Sally looked at Billy, probably trying to understand what was going on. He nodded to her.

"It's okay," he said, afraid she might try to disobey and incur the wrath of Beck. While Billy thought Beck would keep his promise not to kill the lover or child of the sheriff, they all knew Sally had no connection to them whatsoever. "Do as he says," Billy said gently.

Sally, who looked to be in her late sixties, finally moved toward them. She stopped at Billy's other side and looked at Beck.

"Billy, take your gun out and give the clip to Mara," Beck ordered. For the first time, he moved the shotgun. Now it was pointing squarely at Mara. "If you so much as try to take aim at me, I will end this now and you'll lose everyone you love in one fell swoop. So do it now."

Billy did as he was told. He unholstered his gun and ejected the clip. He handed it to Mara. She took it with a slightly shaking hand. He wished he could hold her. Let her know everything was going to be okay.

"Empty the chamber and then give it to our new friend, Sally."

Billy ejected the bullet in the chamber and then handed his service weapon to Sally. She, too, was shaking.

"Now, Sally, I want you to run."

"R-run?" Her face paled considerably.

Beck nodded in the direction from which she'd come.

"I want you to run as fast as you can in that direction and don't stop or come back, or I'll kill these good people. You wouldn't want that on your conscience, now, would you, Sally?"

The woman shook her head. Her eyes began to water.

"Then go!"

Sally began to walk away before picking up the pace, gun in her hand. Billy hoped she didn't hurt herself. He also hoped she had the sense to get help.

"Okay, say *see you soon, Billy*, and let's go," Beck said to Mara.

"I—" Billy started, but Mara interrupted him again.

"I'm going," she said.

Billy took her face back into his hands and brushed

his lips across hers. He hoped the kiss told her everything he couldn't say.

He would save Alexa.

He would save Mara.

He would destroy Beck.

In that order.

"Now, Billy, you know the drill. You move, I end this today. Both of their deaths will be because you tried to be a hero. And ended up protecting no one but yourself. Understood?"

Billy gave a curt nod. Anger flowed through his veins like blood. He'd never wanted another man to come to as much harm as he did the man in front of him.

"I'll get you in the end," Billy promised.

Beck grinned. "I expect you'll try."

Beck walked Mara, shotgun to the back of her neck, away from him. He kept looking back to make sure Billy was still there. Billy made sure not to move an inch. He didn't want to push the already crazed man.

A few people outside the church had finally spotted the procession and, Billy hoped, had called 911. No one moved to help Mara. It angered and also relieved Billy. Instead, they all watched in muted terror, some fleeing back into the church, as Beck angled Mara into a car he'd never seen before, parked right next to Billy's Bronco.

He ground his teeth hard, watching, helpless, as the mother of his child was taken away.

BILLY ROCKETED THROUGH the streets of Carpenter toward his house. He had absolutely no way to contact the world outside of his car. When he'd run back to the Bronco, the driver's side door had been open. His cellphone and radio were gone. Thank God he'd had enough sense to at least keep the car keys in his pocket when he'd followed Mara.

He'd tried, in vain, to keep his eyes on Beck's new car as they left the parking lot, but by the time he'd run to the Bronco, they were gone. It had left Billy with too many options. Too many routes to follow.

Though, if he was being honest with himself, there was really only one place he needed to go.

Chapter Nineteen

Deputy Mills's cruiser was still parked on the street outside the Reed family home. Just like it had been when Billy and Mara had left that morning. However, where Billy had expected chaos on his lawn, shattered house windows and a front door broken off its hinges, all Billy could see was what they'd left behind that morning. Everything looked orderly, calm. *Normal.*

But that didn't ease Billy's mind.

He hit his brakes at the end of the driveway and jumped out, already running to the front door.

"Sheriff," someone yelled from behind him. He turned so fast he nearly fell. It was Deputy Mills, standing in the now-open door of his cruiser. Again, Billy expected him to look one way—angry, wounded from the attack—but he looked another—confused, alert. "What's going on?"

"What happened?" Billy asked. He could tell it put the man further on edge.

"What are you talking about?"

Billy heard the squeal from inside the house. He

didn't wait on the porch to question the deputy. He flung open the front door and ran inside, attention sticking to a sound he hadn't thought he'd hear in the house.

"Don't move," came a growl of a voice. Billy turned in the entry to see a startled Suzy, gun raised.

"Billy? What are you doing?" she asked, surprised. She lowered her gun but didn't put it away.

"Is Alexa here?" he asked, knowing he must have looked crazy. He didn't care.

"Of course she's here." Suzy pointed into the living room. Billy hurried past her, hearing another squeal of laughter.

Sitting on the floor was his mother, alarmed but seemingly unhurt. Plastic containers of Christmas decorations littered the space in front of her. At her side, amid an explosion of toys that nearly rivaled the decorations, was the most beautiful sight Billy had ever seen.

"Alexa!"

The little girl looked up at him, green eyes wide and curious. She had a stuffed dog in her hand. She held it out to him, unaware of the sheer amount of love flooding through Billy from just seeing her.

"Dog," she yelled. It was enough to get him moving.

In two long strides Billy scooped Alexa up and hugged her tight. He might not have been in her life up until this point, but Billy had never been more certain of any one thing in all his life.

He loved his daughter.

He held on to the moment, closing his eyes and burying his face in her hair. Alexa giggled.

That sound of perfect innocence split Billy's heart in two.

Yes, Alexa was safe.

But what about Mara?

Billy kissed Alexa's forehead before putting her back down, a plan already forming in his head. He turned to his mother.

"Pack your bag and one for her, too."

He turned to Suzy and the deputy as Dante hustled through the front door. He didn't talk to them until all three were back in the entryway. Where he promptly punched the wall.

"Billy," he heard his mom exclaim, but Suzy was closer. She holstered her gun.

"What happened?" she asked. "Where's Mara?"

"Beck lied. He took Mara." Billy heard his mother gasp, but he didn't have time to deal with the emotions behind what had happened. "And I let him."

BECK HAD BLINDFOLDED and handcuffed Mara so quickly she hadn't been able to see the person who ended up driving them away from the church and its neighboring park. All Mara knew was that it wasn't Beck. He'd stayed in the back with her, rambling on about how proud he was to finally have her in his possession. And not only that, but he'd also managed to take her from the sheriff himself.

It wasn't surprising to Mara to find out the man

liked to gloat, but that didn't mean that listening wasn't disconcerting.

She tried to keep her nerves as calm as possible by thinking of Alexa. Even if she had no idea what was going on with her little girl, the love Mara felt strengthened her resolve to survive this.

Mara remained quiet for the length of the drive. There were too many questions and she had no way of answering half of them. She couldn't control what Billy was doing, what her daughter was feeling and the fact that she was handcuffed next to someone who was obviously insane. What she *could* do, however, was try and pay attention to how many times the car turned and how long they drove. She might not know the town of Carpenter as thoroughly as Billy, but it couldn't hurt to try and remember as much of the route as possible.

After almost fifteen minutes the smooth road became bumpy, pocked. A few minutes later, they left asphalt altogether. The change in terrain was rough. A dirt road.

Which meant one of two things.

They were either on some back road in Riker County that she didn't know about, or they had left a road altogether and were out in the country.

Mara didn't know which option was better.

"Pull around to the side," Beck said to the driver, giving rise to another question Mara didn't have the answer to. Was the driver the "associate" who had taken her daughter? Was that the same person who'd killed Caleb and Jessica, and wounded Cassie?

Mara tensed as the car slowed and then stopped. The engine remained on.

"Time to go," Beck said, opening his door. Mara sat up, fighting the urge to try and, well, fight—she didn't want to jeopardize Alexa's safety, wherever she might be—and waited until the door next to her was opened. "Stay smart," Beck cooed beside her ear. Mara flinched as he grabbed the handcuff's chain and pulled her out. Once her feet hit the ground, she knew she was standing on grass.

"Stay in the car," Beck ordered his partner. Whoever that was didn't answer. Beck moved his grip from the handcuffs to Mara's upper arm and directed her forward a few feet before turning. In that time, Mara tried to keep her adrenaline in check so she could pay attention once again to her surroundings.

It was colder now, finally starting to feel like Christmas. Though that didn't help Mara narrow down the possibilities of where she might be. But after straining her ears to try to listen around the running car and their footsteps, there was one thing she didn't hear that made her feel even more uneasy.

She didn't hear any other cars.

Which meant they probably *were* in the country, cut off from any normal traffic. Cut off from any easy help. Just plain cut off.

"We're going to go inside and I'm going to take your blindfold off," Beck said at her ear. "If you try to fight me or do anything stupid, I won't kill you, but I'll hurt you really badly. Okay?"

Mara didn't answer. He must have taken her silence as agreement. The sound of a door scrubbing against the floor preceded her being pushed inside a building. She smelled something that was between a wet dog and freshly mowed grass but couldn't pinpoint it any more accurately than that. She didn't have the time, either, before Beck was giving her yet another order.

"Don't move."

The pressure of his hand on her arm went away and soon she could hear him moving something. It scraped against whatever was beneath it, sounding much heavier than a table or chair.

Terror started to seize her chest. Questions and fears shot off in succession in her mind. What was going on? Where were they? What was going to happen to her? Was Beck really not going to kill her? Where was Alexa? Was she scared? Hurt?

Mara jumped as hands moved to the sides of her head. Quick fingers undid the blindfold. She blinked several times, trying to get her bearings. Wherever they were, it was darker than she'd like. Her eyes weren't adjusting quickly enough to make out the location.

"There's a set of stairs behind you," Beck said, motioning for her to turn. "I want you to go down them." Mara looked over her shoulder. The sound she'd heard of something heavy being moved was a large, rectangular canister. It stood next to a hole in the floor.

Not a hole. A trap door.

There was a faint light radiating out of it, but she couldn't tell where it led. She took a second to let her eyes adjust, but still couldn't make out what exactly was down those stairs.

Seeing the trap door and the hidden stairwell might have made some people feel adventurous, but right now, the image only heightened Mara's acute fear of having to walk down them.

Good thing she still had a few questions to ask before she would.

"Where's Alexa?"

Beck cracked a smile. It sent a shiver down her spine. The shotgun he held against his side didn't help.

"She's safe with her dad," he answered. She searched his face, looking for the lie. She was surprised to realize she believed he was being sincere. Besides, if he *had* done something to Alexa, Mara bet he would have been gloating about it.

And she would have already killed him with her bare hands.

Plus, there wasn't much more to do than believe him and hope Billy was doing everything he could to ensure Alexa stayed safe. She had little doubt he would do anything else.

Just thinking about the two of them, without her in the picture, warmed and broke Mara's heart. Despair at potentially never seeing them again inspired her backbone to stiffen. Suddenly, the danger of the man across from her lessened. Mara had much bigger things to fear than a man who had to threaten a toddler to get what he wanted.

"You do know I have no idea where the drugs and

money are, right?" Mara asked, pleased at the steadiness of her voice. She raised her chin a fraction to show the man she was above lying to him. Why waste her time doing it?

For one moment, Mara felt like she had the upper hand. Like she had stumped the man who had been nothing but cocky. But then the moment was shattered.

All it took was one smirk to let Mara know she hadn't won.

"I believe you," he said, seeming amused.

"What?"

Beck gave a little chuckle.

"I know you don't have any idea where the stash is," he continued. "In fact, I've known for a bit."

Mara was dumbfounded.

"Then why come after me?" she asked. "Why go through all of this trouble to get me if I can't even help?"

Beck's smirk stayed sharp when he answered, as if he'd been waiting for those questions for a while and it was finally time for him to deliver.

"Because now I have the only leverage in all the world that would make your father finally tell me where it is."

Mara couldn't help it. She laughed. It wasn't in the least kind.

"Good luck with that. My father wouldn't help me when I asked for it. What makes you think he'll help you now, just because you have me?"

"Because I'm not bartering for your release. I'm

bartering for your life," Beck said simply. "You aren't leaving this place alive unless your father does everything I need him to, what I told the sheriff earlier be damned. He's a handsome fella, though, so don't worry. I'm sure he can find another woman to get into his bed and raise your kid if you're gone."

The shiver that had run down Mara's spine before was back with a vengeance. It crippled any confidence she'd been wielding as a shield against her current situation. And the madman across from her. The strength that had kept her voice steady was gone when she answered.

"My father won't help you," she said.

"You'd be surprised what a father will do for his daughter." He brought the shotgun up and pointed it at her. "Now, get down there, Miss Copeland," he ordered. "I've got things to do."

The last thing Mara wanted to do was go down those steps. To find out where that dim light was and what the destination might mean for her future. But Mara couldn't deny that she felt deflated. She'd done what she could and now she might have to let whatever was going to happen play out.

Without another look at her captor, Mara started the descent down the stairs. She was less than four steps in when the door above her was dragged closed. She waited as the sound of the metal scraping filled the air. Something heavy went on top of the trap door. Mara backtracked until she could put her shoulders and back against it. She tried to push up, but the door didn't budge.

Letting out an exhale of defeat, she started her descent again.

The stairs weren't as long as she'd expected, and soon she was standing in a surprisingly large room lit by two hanging bulbs. They cast enough light to reach the corners.

Which was good and bad for Mara.

It was good because she could tell with certainty that she was standing in a basement, maybe used as a storage room at some point, judging by the lumps of furniture covered by dust cloths and pushed against the walls. And knowing *where* she was felt a lot better than sitting in the dark, wondering.

However, for every silver lining there was something bad that had to be coped with, and tied in a chair against the wall was a woman who looked like she'd seen a heck of a lot better days.

"Leigh?" Mara started, beyond confused.

Leigh Cullen had her mouth taped over and blood on her face. She looked just as surprised to see Mara as Mara was to see her.

That, in itself, would have been enough to make a terrifying situation even more dark, but then Mara noticed the boy in the corner, tied to an old oak rocking chair. His mouth was duct taped, his eyes wide. He didn't look much older than ten.

What the hell was going on?

Chapter Twenty

Mara rocked backward on the floor so that her knees were in the air. Before she'd had Alexa she could have gotten the handcuffs from behind her back to in front of herself without much fuss, but since she'd given birth and become a single parent, her exercise habits had disappeared. That included the yoga routine that had kept her flexible. As it was, it took several tries before she was able to get her hands in front of her. They were still bound, but at least now she could use them.

Her maternal instincts had gone from zero to a hundred the moment she'd seen the boy. She didn't recognize him. Still, she hurried over to him with the most soothing voice she could muster.

"Hey, there, my name's Mara," she started, honey coating every syllable. "I'm going to take the tape off your mouth. Is that okay?" The boy, short brown hair, freckles galore and wide blue eyes already filling up with tears, cut his gaze to Leigh. The woman, in turn, slit her eyes at Mara. "I'm not with them, Leigh. A man named Beck took me and brought me here."

It was the vaguest of answers but seemed enough to satisfy the woman. She nodded to the boy. He looked back at Mara and nodded.

"This might hurt a little, but I'll try to be extra gentle," she warned him.

The boy gave another curt nod. He closed his eyes tight as Mara got a grip on the edge of the tape and did her best to ease it off without causing the boy pain. No sooner had it passed over his lips did he give a cry of relief. It made Mara's heart squeeze.

"You did so good," Mara said, knowing the tears in his eyes were a thin dam away from being an all-out waterfall. "I'm going to try and untie you now, and then you can help me untie her." The boy nodded, sniffling. Mara went to the side of the chair and then to the back trying to find the main knot. Thankfully, it wasn't too complicated, resting at the base of the chair. Then again, the boy was small enough that he probably didn't need much help keeping him tied down. "So, what's your name?"

"Eric," he said, tears behind his words. "Er-Eric Cullen."

"Leigh's your mama," she guessed.

"Yes, ma'am."

She'd known that Leigh had a kid, but what had happened with her husband had always taken priority in Mara's mind. A swell of guilt rose at the realization that she'd never even asked after the boy, but Mara batted it down. She needed to focus. And she needed to try and calm Eric down. Even from her crouched position behind him, she could see he was trembling.

"So, Eric, what grade are you in?" she asked, working on undoing the first part of the knot.

"Fo-fourth."

"Oh, nice! That's a fun grade. So you have any favorite classes you're looking forward to after Christmas break?"

The first part of the knot gave way. There were two more to go.

"I like practicing football," he said flatly. "But Mama says I can't play on the team if I don't bring up my grades."

The second part fell away. Mara found herself smiling at his answer.

"I'd have to agree with her there," she said.

He nodded but didn't say anything else. Mara wanted to know how they'd gotten down here and what had happened to them, but she didn't want to push the little guy to relive whatever they'd gone through. She'd just have to ask his mama instead.

"Okay, there we go."

Mara stood, wincing as the pain in her side reminded her she should have been resting, and helped take the rope from around him.

"You okay?" Mara asked.

He nodded but she helped him stand all the same. Another part of her heart squeezed when she noticed a bruise on the side of his face. Like he'd been hit.

"Now, you think you can help me untie her?"

Leigh's eyes were shining but she didn't cry when Mara took the tape off her mouth.

"Oh, Eric, are you okay?" were the first words

out of her mouth. The boy's chin started to tremble but he nodded.

Mara let him stand in front of his mom while she checked him over, uttering assurances that they'd all be alright, while she jumped into untying Leigh. The ropes had more knots, including at her ankles and wrists. Judging by the blood and marks all over the woman, Mara'd bet she'd put up one heck of a fight before they'd been able to get her tied down.

"This might take a little bit," Mara said, fingers fumbling with the knot at the back of her chair. "So let's not waste any time. What the heck is going on? And where are we?"

"We're at the house," Eric said, matter-of-factly.

"The house?"

"We're in a barn," Leigh clarified. "It's on my family's farm. Our house is a mile in that direction."

She nodded to the right wall.

"And this charming little room?" Mara asked, fingers tugging at another knot.

"My great-grandfather put it in to serve as a storm shelter of sorts. It's always creeped me out, so we never come out here. Until today." Leigh said a string of curses before apologizing to her son for doing just that. A heavy sigh followed. "I wanted an old picture of the main house my daddy took when he was a boy that's in one of these boxes. I was going to reframe it as a present for him. Lucky for us, it just happened to be the same day two thugs decided to camp out in the barn. They surprised us after I opened the trap door."

There it was again.

The swelling of guilt. This time Mara didn't let it sit and stew.

This time she let it out.

"It's my fault they're here," she admitted. "They're trying to use me to get something that's hidden somewhere in Riker County."

Mara didn't need to be looking at the woman to know she wasn't happy.

"Eric, why don't you go look for that picture?" Leigh said quietly. "It should be in one of those boxes."

Eric must have known his mom's tones. He obeyed without hesitation, walking across the room from them and pulling off a dust cloth. Mara undid the back knot and was in front of Leigh when the woman had collected herself enough to respond.

"It's about that no-good father of yours, isn't it?" she whispered, low and angry.

Mara nodded. She tried to get into a better position to work on the ropes holding Leigh's ankles to the legs of the chair. Pain flashed up her side again.

"What's wrong?" Leigh asked. Her eyes trailed to the bruise on Mara's head.

"Let's just say I've had a long day," she hedged.

Leigh kept quiet as Mara finished untying her. Such a seemingly simple task had left her exhausted. Instead of jumping up, as the now-free woman did, she pushed her back up against the wall and sat down. All the adrenaline spikes she'd had that day were long past gone. Now Mara felt pain and weariness.

She watched in silence as Leigh ran to her son and nearly crushed him in a hug.

Mara smiled. Pain aside, she'd give Alexa the same greeting.

If she ever saw her again.

BILLY HUGGED HIS mother and kissed his daughter's cheek.

"Are you sure there's no other way? We could just keep all the doors locked and maybe—"

"Mom."

Billy's mother let her arguments go and nodded to her son. She had Alexa on her hip, the diaper bag on her arm and pure concern on her face. But she wasn't going to argue anymore. Time was a luxury they had little of.

"You be careful," she said instead. "And bring her back."

"I will."

She touched the side of his face before giving him and Suzy some privacy. Alexa waved at him, although her eyes trailed between all the adults in the house. She'd been surprisingly quiet since he'd arrived. It made Billy wonder if she was looking for Mara among everyone. It was a good thing she'd taken such a shine to his mother, or else the next step in his plan wouldn't go over as well as they wanted.

"I don't like this," Suzy said, coming to stand in front of him. She met and held his eyes.

"I know, but it needs to be done."

"And you're not asking me just because I'm a woman, right?"

Billy returned the serious question with an equal answer.

"You know damn well it's not that," he said. Still, he saw some doubt there. He tried to diminish it as quickly as he could. "Beck played me like a fiddle just by talking about Alexa. I can't afford to let him do that again, so I need to *know* that she'll be okay. Which means I need someone I trust. Not only with my life, but with my mother's and child's lives, too. Like it or not, that's you, Suze. None of this will work if you're not the one to take them out of town and hide them." He gave her a small smile. "I'm asking as the little boy you once called dumb as nails for tanking the spelling bee in fourth grade. Not as your sheriff."

That seemed to soften the woman. She let out a sigh before her shoulders pushed back. She raised her chin. Not out of pride. It was determination.

"Who misspells elephant?" She smirked and then was deadly serious. "Go get your gal, Sheriff."

And then Suzy was gone, her own bag slung across her shoulder. No one knew how long it would take to find Mara and stop Beck, but Suzy wasn't bringing Alexa or his mother back until both happened.

Billy just hoped that was sooner rather than later.

Dane met Billy in the lobby the moment he walked in. He looked impeccable, letting Billy know he'd already done the press conference. Which he confirmed with his greeting.

"The public should be on the lookout for Beck and

his associate, and both the car they drove away in and the truck they had earlier, too. Mara's picture is also out there. Dante is briefing the reserve deputies who just came in, while we have some of our deputies manning the tip lines and social media. The rest, including the local PD, are out on the streets and in the country."

"And no bites yet?" Billy asked, already knowing the answer.

Dane shook his head.

"Nothing we didn't already know. But I think Matt's ready to talk to us about what he's found on Beck's friend."

Billy nodded and they headed deeper into the building.

"Let's hope we finally have a lead."

BILLY STOOD AT the front of the squad room and looked out at his deputies. Those who were close by had been asked to come in. Those on patrol were being filled in on the new situation in person by Mills and one of the reserve deputies. Because the radios were now a problem.

A bigger one than they already had.

"Gene Marsden worked at Riker County Sheriff's Department for twelve years before he was fired by the last sheriff," Billy started. "There was a list a mile long of reasons why he should have been let go sooner but Sheriff Rockwell liked giving second—and sometimes third—chances to his deputies because he knew that this job can be a hard one. But then, when we were working the Bryan Copeland case, Rockwell noticed that crime scenes and evidence were being tampered with on Marsden's watch. He never found concrete proof that it was Marsden. but after a late night of drinking at a local bar, Marsden started to brag about having his own personal collection of Moxy. Courtesy of the department. He was fired as Rockwell's last act as sheriff, and when he came to me to rehire him, I flat out said no." Billy crossed his arms over his chest. "To put it bluntly, he lost his damn mind."

Two deputies sitting in the back agreed, using more colorful language. Billy pointed to them. Along with Dane and Matt, they'd been present for the scene. "He had to be escorted out. After that, he moved to Georgia, where his sister lives, and didn't make so much as a peep." Billy gave Matt a nod.

The detective cleared his throat to address the room.

"Until two months ago, when he apparently came back." Matt pinned the picture of Marsden they'd been able to get from the security camera at the local bar, the Eagle. "The owner of the Eagle said Marsden has been paying in cash only. One night he got so drunk they called him a cab, which took him to the same hotel where the recently deceased Caleb Richards had been meeting Beck. Around the same time Beck fled, Marsden disappeared."

"We think he might have a police radio, which is why they've always been right there with us every step of the investigation," Billy added. "Even though it was checked in when he was fired, we can't find it." Just saying the words made Billy angrier than he already was.

"Is that the only evidence we have on him? Coming back to town, staying in the same hotel and hating you?" one of the reserve deputies asked. The question might have seemed like the man was unimpressed but Billy knew he was just a straight shooter. He wanted all the information they had before trying to bring down a former cop.

Which brought Billy to a crossroads.

He could tell his deputies to trust him right then and there without any more information and they would. Maybe.

Or Billy could follow Mara's earlier example in the park.

He could finally tell the truth.

"Mara Copeland and I became involved during the case against her father." He didn't wait for any reactions. "After he was convicted, we were going to go public with the relationship but Mara was approached by Marsden, who had found out about us. He threatened Mara with the idea that I would lose my career because of her. So she left." The words tasted bitter in his mouth but Billy continued. "Only a handful of people knew about Mara and I, and none of them have since told. When I talked to Beck, he already knew about the relationship, making me believe Marsden had found out by overhearing Bryan Copeland talking to me about it the day we arrested him." Billy readjusted his stance. When he spoke again he could hear the hardness in his voice. The bottom line. "While it might not be professional, I love Mara Copeland a whole hell of a lot. That goes double for our daughter."

A few surprised looks swept over the deputies' faces but no one stopped him. "That might not be reason enough to warrant us going after a former cop considering, you're right, we don't have anything concrete to tie him to Beck, but Marsden is the best lead we have. We track Marsden, there's a good chance we find Beck. We find Beck, we find Mara. And if any of you have any reservations about this, well…" Billy paused a second to work up a smirk. "Too bad for you. Because I'm the sheriff and this is an order."

He'd been waiting for some opposition, so Billy was surprised when none came. The men and women sitting in front of him all seemed to agree with gusto.

In fact, some even cheered.

"Alright, let's get to work!"

Chapter Twenty-One

"Why were you at the sheriff's department the other day?" Mara finally thought to ask Leigh.

She let her gaze linger on the picture of Alexa she'd had in her pocket before putting it back. According to Leigh's watch they'd been in the basement for more than three hours. In that time Mara had told the woman everything that had happened, including her part in taking her father down. Something that might not have softened the woman toward her but did seem to surprise her.

The fact of the matter was that Leigh's husband was still dead because of the Copelands. Something she was reminded of every time she looked at Eric, who had finally fallen asleep in the corner. While Mara had been there for a few hours, Leigh and Eric had been there since that morning. The stress of it had been exhausting for the boy.

Mara couldn't blame him. If the need to escape hadn't been so great, she might have tried to get a few minutes of shut-eye herself.

Leigh stopped looking in the box in front of her and turned, already scowling. She motioned to Eric.

"While I was at the grocery store, some man showed up at the house asking all sorts of weird questions," she said. "When Eric asked what his name was, the man refused to tell him. After he left, Eric called me. I was already near the department so I thought I'd drop in."

Mara was about to dismiss Leigh's story when a cold thought slid into her head.

"What did the man look like?"

Leigh pursed her lips, still not happy being stuck in the basement with Mara, but she answered.

"Eric said he was really tall, had brown hair cut really close, almost like what the army fellows wear, looked around his Uncle Daniel's age—midforties— and, not so much like his uncle, he was skinny. Why?"

Mara let out a sigh of relief. Definitely not Beck. She was about to say as much when another terrible thought pushed in. The knot that had sunk to the bottom of her stomach began to spawn other knots.

"What questions did he ask?"

The man might not have been Beck but that didn't mean she didn't recognize the description.

Leigh must have read the fear in her expression. She dropped the contempt she'd been treating Mara with and answered.

"He asked if we'd had any construction done two or three years ago and, if so, where." The knots in Mara's stomach turned cold. Her heart rate started to pick up. "But, of course, all Eric could think about was his dad being killed two years ago, so he said he didn't know. Then he asked if Eric was home alone and, thank God, he lied. That's when he asked what the man's name was and he left."

Mara nearly missed the end of Leigh's sentence. Her thoughts were racing alongside her heart now.

"Leigh, *did* you have any construction done in the last three years? Anyone coming in and out of the property with trucks or trailers?"

Leigh's eyebrow rose but she nodded.

"Right after my husband passed. We had a bad storm blow through. It flung a tree over and messed up the roof." She pointed up, meaning the barn's roof. "Had a company come in to replace it. They were really nice, too. Cut me a deal on account of being a recent widow. Even planted a new tree near the barn and left a note saying I could watch it and Eric grow up together. I thought it was really sweet. Okay, Mara, what is it? You look like you've seen a ghost."

Mara felt like it, too.

"My father hid a stash of drugs and money right before he went to court, as a fail-safe. We thought that there was a possibility that he used construction as a way to help him hide it, but we've only looked one place. The high school." Mara was struck with such a strong realization that a laugh escaped between her lips. "I never would have *ever* thought to look here. The guilt of what happened to you—to your family— would have made me, and maybe Billy, too, never even think to come here. And my father knew that. It's the perfect place."

Mara shook her head again, but she felt like she was right.

"Leigh, I think my dad's stash is here."

"But you said Beck was still looking for it," Leigh pointed out.

"That's just it. I don't think Beck even knows. I think he picked this place because it's remote and he knows only you and Eric live here. You probably would have never noticed them had you not wanted that picture."

Leigh's face contorted into an emotion that Mara was sure was laced with more than a few colorful words, when a scraping sound cut through the air. Someone was moving the canister off the trap door. It made Mara remember the original thought she'd had.

"I think that man who talked to Eric was Gene Marsden," Mara hurried while she and Leigh retreated to Eric. Mara paused and then switched directions. She grabbed an old lamp she'd pulled from a box earlier and pointed to the vintage baseball bat Leigh had found. "And if he's found out the stash is here, I think he'll kill us."

WHEN IT RAINED, it poured.

That was Billy's first thought when his office received a call from an unknown number. He didn't know what to expect, but he thought it wouldn't be good. So when the caller turned out to be Bryan Copeland, Billy was more than a little thrown.

"I told Beck where the stash was," he started.

"You what?" Billy rocked out of his chair, already spitting mad.

Bryan didn't seem bothered by his anger. In fact, he seemed to be harboring his own.

"The deal was Mara's life for the location." Bryan went on. "Apparently, I still love my daughter. Now, you got a pen?"

Billy wrote down the address Bryan rattled off and couldn't help but be surprised by it but didn't have the time to say so. He also didn't have the time to ask what number the man was calling from or how Beck had gotten hold of him. Those were issues he'd tackle later.

"Now hurry, Sheriff, and go save the girl. I don't believe for a second this Beck will let her go alive," Bryan said, already cutting the conversation short. Billy almost didn't hear it when he tacked on a last question. "And, Billy, is Alexa safe?"

While he had no reason in the world to answer the man, Billy did.

"Yeah, she's safe."

"Good."

Bryan ended the call. Seconds later, Billy was out the door.

No SOONER HAD Beck walked off the last step than Mara smashed the lamp against his head. He made a wild noise as the glass shattered against him, but the wrath of the women he'd imprisoned wasn't finished. Mara slid to the side as Leigh swung her bat for all she was worth into his crotch.

Beck never had a chance.

He hit the ground hard and didn't move. The shotgun he'd been holding thunked next to him. It was closer to Leigh, so she scurried to grab it while Mara readied for the next bad guy, hoping she could still do damage even though her grip was off thanks to the handcuffs.

But no one came.

The two of them froze and listened.

"I don't hear anything," Mara whispered.

"Maybe Marsden isn't here?"

"Let's not just stand here and wait to find out."

Leigh nodded, but hesitated.

"Have you ever shot a gun?" she asked, motioning to the shotgun in her hands.

"Not one of those."

Leigh gritted her teeth.

"I'll hold on to it, then," she said. "Follow me up. Eric, get behind Mara."

Eric crawled out from his hiding spot in the corner and listened to his mom. He stood behind Mara and kept his eyes off Beck.

"Wait, he's got a phone on him!"

Mara saw the light from his pocket as his cell phone vibrated. Leigh trained the shotgun on him as Mara fished the phone out. The caller ID was *M.*

"Marsden," Leigh guessed.

"Which means he's probably not up there?"

The thought got them moving. Mara held the phone, careful not to answer it, and followed Leigh up the stairs while Eric held on to the back of her shirt. If Marsden wasn't in the barn, then there was a good chance they'd be able to get to the house. She could even use Beck's cell phone to call for help once Marsden stopped calling. If he didn't know they had escaped, Mara definitely wasn't going to let him know by answering the phone.

Leigh moved slowly when she ascended, shotgun swiveling side to side, until she was out of view. Mara held her breath, waiting for the go-ahead. Her heart was hammering in her ears.

"We're alone," Leigh whispered down to them after what felt like hours.

Mara, relieved for the dose of good news, led Eric up the stairs. The air smelled musty and damp. The sun that had barely lit the space earlier in the day was gone. Like the basement, there were sets of hanging bulbs. They hung from the rafters, looking tired and weak. The light they emitted wasn't anything to write home about, but Mara welcomed it all the same. At least she could see. A silver lining to the nightmare the day had turned into.

"The house is a mile that way," Leigh whispered, pointing to the wall on their right. "Call your sheriff and tell him we're headed there. I have a lot more guns in that house than I bet Marsden brought to town." Despite their strained, nearly nonexistent relationship, Mara found herself grateful that out of all the women she could have been held captive with, Beck had been stupid enough to pick Leigh Cullen.

Mara fumbled with the phone and dialed 911 with her cuffed hand, ready to tell the dispatcher as quickly as possible everything that was happening and get Billy sent their way. Because they were out of Carpenter's town limits, the call should go straight to the Riker County Sheriff's Department instead of the local police. Which meant Billy would get to them faster.

Get to *her* faster.

That thought alone put some pep in her step. The idea of seeing Billy after everything that had happened was more than a desire to Mara. Now it was a need. As real and essential as breathing. She needed Billy Reed.

Sitting in the basement for hours had given her more than enough time to think about the sheriff. While she'd known that he would keep Alexa in his life now that he knew about her, Mara didn't know where that left the two of them.

Would they coparent from two different homes? Two different towns?

The mere idea of being away from Billy tore through Mara with surprising ferocity. For two years it had been only her and Alexa. But now that Mara remembered what having Billy around again was like, could she go back to living a life without him by her side?

Going through boxes of Leigh's family's antiques, Mara had realized that, no, she couldn't. She didn't want to go back to a house that didn't have the sheriff between its walls. She didn't want to take Alexa away from her father anymore, not even for the briefest of moments. For the first time in years, Mara had come to a realization so poignant that she'd nearly cried right there in the basement.

Two years ago, she should have fought for Billy— for *them*—instead of running.

She wasn't going to make the same mistake again.

However, Mara never found out how fast her 911 call would have reached the sheriff. Before she could hit the send button, the door in the corner of the barn was flung open.

Mara recognized the former cop, Gene Marsden, as easily as she'd heard his words at the ceremony years ago. He hadn't changed in the time since, matching Eric's description to a T, but the gun he was carrying definitely wasn't police issue. He pointed it at Leigh so quickly that it didn't seem humanly possible.

"I'll kill you first," he warned. His voice was steady, calm. It made his threat all the more believable. So much so that Leigh didn't shoot. Which probably was for the best, since there were several feet between them. If she'd missed...

"Kick the gun over here," he ordered before looking at Mara. "And toss the phone this way, too. You call anyone and I'll shoot the boy in the head."

Eric pulled on her shirt a little and she immediately did as she was told. The same went for Leigh. Even if it meant giving up the only upper hand they had. There were just some chances you didn't take. Especially when you believed the threat if you failed.

One look at Marsden's grin and Mara believed his every word.

"Now, back into the basement," he said, using his gun to make a shooing motion at them. Mara shared a look with Leigh. He didn't miss it. "I'll kill the boy, remember?"

"We're going," Mara said quickly. She put the trembling boy in front of her and followed him back into what was becoming Mara's least favorite place in the entire world.

Beck was still lying on the floor and, for a moment, she wondered if he was dead. It wasn't until they had all stepped over him and were in the middle of the room that he let out a low groan.

"You let two women and some little kid get the better of you," Marsden said, showing nothing but disgust for his partner. "How can you live with yourself?" If Beck tried to answer, Mara couldn't tell. The lamp had cut his face up something awful. Blood ran down it like a fountain. It was almost too much to look at, but Marsden seemed to have no trouble sneering at him. "You know, some men would take their lives rather than lose their dignity," Marsden drawled. "But I already know you'd never have the jewels to do that." Marsden took a step back and pointed his gun down. "So I'll do it for you."

And then he shot Beck in the head.

Chapter Twenty-Two

Eric was crying.

Mara wanted to join him.

Killing someone in cold blood was enough to terrify any witness. Killing your partner in cold blood was downright bone-chilling.

"Don't worry, I was going to do that anyways," Marsden said. "Beck liked to talk a lot, but words aren't street smarts. I don't know how he planned to make this business idea of his work." He looked at Mara expectantly.

"You—you mean bringing Moxy back to Riker County," she guessed when he didn't look away.

Marsden laughed.

"I don't think as small as Beck here does." He paused, then corrected himself. "Or did." Mara kept her eyes on Marsden and not the growing puddle of blood around the man he was so casually dismissing. She wondered if he could hear her heart trying to ram itself clear out of her body.

Marsden took a moment to give each of them an appraising look. It made Leigh move so that Eric was hidden behind her completely. If he was offended, he didn't comment on it.

"Now, here's the deal," he said when no one made a peep. What were they supposed to say? Mara had no idea what he knew or what he planned to do with them. "Unlike Beck here, I'm not going to bore you with nonstop chatter and I expect the same from you." He pointed to Mara then thrust his thumb back to the stairs. Panic jolted through her, rooting her to the spot. "You're coming with me."

"Why?" she couldn't help but ask. As much as she disliked the basement, going anywhere alone with Marsden was worse.

"We've got treasure to dig up, that's why." He pointed his gun at Leigh's head. Eric's crying intensified. "They're only alive because of you right now. If you fight me, I'll kill them."

"Why are you doing this?" Mara cried out. The question seemed to amuse him. He actually laughed.

"For money, what else?" That one little laugh sounded twisted. Marsden had lost his patience. "Now, move it or I kill the boy first."

Mara didn't hesitate this time. She never wanted to be the cause of pain for the Cullens again. She didn't want to be the reason Leigh lost her son or Eric lost his mother.

Mara straightened her back, held up her chin and started to walk. It wasn't until she was outside and looking at the flat, open area between the barn and the woods that her confidence faded.

Her thoughts flew to her daughter, who she prayed

was safe, and then to the man who had given her Alexa.

Mara's heart squeezed.

She should have told Billy she still loved him.

And always would.

BILLY RACED ACROSS Leigh Cullen's property in the Bronco cussing. He led a stream of deputies while the local SWAT team was fifteen minutes behind.

He didn't have time to wait for them. While Billy thought Beck might hold off on killing Mara after Bryan had finally given up the location of the stash, he knew that Marsden wouldn't. He was a greedy man with a power complex. And a former cop. He knew firsthand how witnesses and loose ends could undo even the smartest man's plans.

"Marsden won't go down easily," Matt said from the passenger's seat. He had his gun in his hand, ready. "I can't say the same for Beck. I don't know what kind of man he is."

"He likes to talk," Billy said. "If you need to stall, ask him a question about humanity or the line between right or wrong or if he's an Auburn or Alabama fan. I'm sure that'll get him rattling on for a while." Matt snorted. "But you're right about Marsden. If he doesn't have an escape plan set up, he'll make one. And if he can't escape…" Billy didn't finish the thought out loud but they both knew Marsden would kill Mara and Leigh and her kid. As soon as Bryan had told them the stash was next to the barn, marked by a tree that had been planted when he'd brought the cache in, the department had tried to track the Cullens down. Turned out they were missing. Billy only hoped they were still alive, held captive with Mara.

Who also needed to still be alive.

Just the thought of the alternative made Billy cuss some more. It didn't help that in the distance they could just make out a faint light on what must have been the barn. Billy knew Riker County and he'd been out to the Cullens once before, but he didn't know this part of their property. He didn't like the added disadvantage.

"Picked one hell of a night for a showdown," Matt said, leaning forward to look up at the sky. Clouds blanketed the moon and stars. Being out in the country, with no light from above, put them at a further disadvantage. But it at least helped with the next part of Billy's plan.

He slowed and pulled into the grass. Matt radioed the men behind them to do the same. While taking Beck and Marsden by force would be easier, Billy had a feeling it ran the best chance of ending in blood. It was time to rely on stealth.

"Ready?" Matt asked after he checked his gun again. Billy did the same. There was no room to make mistakes.

"Let's finally put an end to this."

There was half a football field's length of flat grass and dirt between them and the barn. An outdoor light hung over one of the doors but it didn't worry Billy. He could make out the outline of a vehicle tucked against the side of the barn they were sneaking toward. Billy'd bet dollars to donuts it was the car Mara had been taken in earlier that day. He knew Beck and Marsden were there. He just didn't know if they were in the barn or on the other side of it.

And he didn't know where Mara was, either.

Billy let his questions shut off as he made it close enough to confirm it was the car he'd seen before. He and Matt stepped quietly while looking in the front and back seats. Then, together, they remained quiet and listened.

The Southern lullaby of cicadas and frogs held steady around them, as normal as the humidity and as loyal to the South as football fans to the game. Billy wouldn't have even noticed the song if he hadn't been trying to hear through it. So when an odd noise went against the natural grain of sound, he tilted his head in confusion.

Matt heard it, too.

"Other side of the barn," he whispered, so quietly Billy barely heard him. But he agreed.

Billy led them along the outer wall, away from the side with the light. He held his breath and kept his body loose as he took a look around the corner. Nothing but more grass, open space and a small amount of clutter lining the back wall of the barn. Even before Leigh had lost her husband, the barn hadn't been used for several years. That fact was merely highlighted when Billy and Matt crept past a door that was heavily chained shut.

They weren't going to be getting anyone in or out that way.

The weird noise Billy couldn't place stopped as soon as they cleared the door. In tandem both men froze at the corner of the barn, guns high and ready.

"I took your cuffs off. You shouldn't be stalling anymore," a man said, loud and clearly frustrated. Billy knew instantly the voice belonged to Gene Marsden. Like nails on a chalkboard, his one sentence was enough to grate on Billy's nerves.

"My ribs are bruised, no thanks to you. If I'm going slow you can thank yourself for that."

Billy could have sung right then and there. Mara was alive.

"You've got a lot of mouth for someone standing in a hole that could be their grave." Billy's joy at hearing Mara's voice plummeted straight down into the fiery depths of pure anger.

No one talked like that to his woman.

"Cover me," he whispered to Matt. He didn't need to see the detective to know he nodded.

Billy crouched, kept his gun straight and swung around the corner of the barn. When bullets didn't fly, he took in several details at once.

There was an old tractor with a flat tire sitting a few feet from the barn's side. Two battery-powered lanterns sat on the ground on the other side of the tractor, casting wide circles of light over two figures. One was Marsden, tall and holding something—a gun, most likely—while Mara was farther away. She was holding a shovel and standing in a hole up to her knees. Next to Marsden was Beck's truck, looking the worse for wear. Neither Marsden nor Mara was directly facing Billy, so he took a beat to look for Beck, Leigh or Eric. When he didn't see anyone else, he started to move toward the back of the tractor.

He could have shot Marsden right then and there—and been happy about it, too—but Mara was too close to the ex-deputy. Billy needed a cleaner shot or a better angle to force the man to disarm himself. Then any chance of that went out the window. Without the lantern's light going past the skeleton of metal, Billy didn't see the beer bottles on the ground until it was too late. His foot connected with one and sent it flying into the other. They sounded off like church bells on a Sunday.

And Marsden didn't waste any time second-guessing the noise. He turned and started shooting.

"Drop your gun, Marsden," Billy yelled after lunging behind the wheel of the tractor. Bullets hit the metal and wood around him, but Marsden didn't answer. He kept Billy pinned down for a few shots until Matt responded to the man in kind. The sounds of gunfire shifted as Marsden must have taken cover behind the truck to take aim at Matt.

"Mara," Billy yelled out, worried she'd be hit in the process. There wasn't any cover she could take easily.

"Billy!"

Like magic Mara appeared around the front of the tractor, seemingly unharmed. There were so many things he wanted to do to her right then and there—appropriate and not so much—but it wasn't the time or place. So he swallowed his desires and got down to business.

"Where's Beck?"

Mara shook her head.

"Dead," she said. "Marsden shot him in the basement." Her eyes widened. "Eric and Leigh are down there still. I need to get them."

The exchange of bullets ceased. Billy bet everyone was reloading.

"You get down there and stay with them," Billy said hurriedly. "Backup is down the road. We'll call them in if you'll stay there."

Mara nodded and turned her body, ready to run, but hesitated. She found his gaze again.

"I never stopped loving you, Billy Reed," she said, voice completely calm. "I promise I'll never leave you again."

Billy, caught more off guard than when the gunfire started up again, didn't have time to respond. Mara didn't wait but kept low, using the tractor as a shield, and soon disappeared around the front of the barn. He heard what must have been the door they'd been using to get in and out of the structure.

The sound shook him from the moment. Billy took a beat to call in their backup and then yelled out to Marsden.

"You're outnumbered," he yelled out. "Put the gun down, Marsden! It's over!"

The shooting stopped again. Billy waited a moment before sticking his head out around the tractor's tire, gun ready. Had Marsden listened to him? Would it be that easy?

"Grenade!"

The two syllables Matt yelled were enough to spike Billy's adrenaline and get him moving, but it wasn't enough time to clear it. He saw the flash-bang arc through the air in the space between him and Matt. Billy dove as far away from it as he could before a deafening blast went off behind him.

The flash blinded him; the sound stunned him.

For several seconds Billy tried to regain some control of his body, his balance, his senses. But before he could, Marsden went for the only option he had left to possibly get out of this mess alive.

Mara.

IT TOOK MARA longer than she would have liked to push the metal canister off the trap door, but she eventually managed.

"It's me," Mara yelled, hands going up to cover her face seconds before Leigh could pummel her with the bat she'd beaten Beck with. His body was still at the bottom of the stairs, in a puddle of blood. Mara jumped over it as Leigh backed away to the side again. Eric popped up from his hiding spot against the wall.

"What's going on up there?" Leigh asked, not dropping the bat to her side.

"Billy showed up." Mara couldn't help but smile. "He told us to stay here. Backup is down the road."

Mara saw the relief in Leigh's shoulders. She leaned the bat against the wall.

"I guess our friend isn't surrendering," she said as more *thunks* could be heard from above.

Mara wrung her hands and shook her head.

"He's definitely not su—"

"Grenade!"

Mara flinched backward and put her hand to her mouth. She gasped as a loud *bang* shook the barn above them. Leigh shared a look with her, eyes wide, as silence filled the world above the basement stairs.

"No," Mara said, shaking her head and still back-pedaling. Surely it was Billy who had thrown it, right? He'd had enough of Marsden and thrown a grenade to end it?

Even as Mara thought it, she knew that wasn't the case.

"Is it over?" Eric asked, bringing her attention to the fact she was at the back wall. Her hand still over her mouth, she didn't have the will to pretend to look like everything was okay.

She wouldn't do that until Billy came down those stairs.

"Should we—" Leigh started. She was cut off by the sound of footsteps coming down into the basement. Mara dropped her hand, a smile coming to her lips thinking of Billy. It was because of that smile that Leigh dropped her guard.

And that's why she didn't beat Marsden to a pulp as soon as his feet hit the floor.

Instead, when she belatedly tried to do some damage, Marsden hauled off and pistol-whipped her. Eric yelled as the force of the hit made Leigh sink to the floor. All she had time to do was look up as Marsden brought up his gun and pointed it at her son.

"For that, I'll kill him before I kill you," he sneered. He looked at Mara. "And then we're leaving."

Mara didn't have time to tell the man that she had no intention of leaving with him.

So, instead, she showed him.

With nothing but the image of Alexa firmly planted in her mind, Mara jumped in front of Eric just as Marsden fired.

BILLY RAN DOWN into the basement and shot Gene Marsden in the head.

His ears rang something awful, his movements were still sluggish and he was having trouble seeing, but none of that could hide one horrifying fact.

Marsden had created Billy's worst nightmare.

He'd shot Mara and he'd done it seconds before Billy could stop him.

"Mara's been shot," he yelled back to Matt.

She was on the ground with Eric standing behind her, crying.

"Are you okay?" Billy yelled at him even though he knew the boy was. Where Mara was lying on her side, it was obvious she'd taken the bullet for the boy. Eric nodded just as Leigh swooped in and grabbed him. They gave Billy space while he dropped down to his knees.

"Mara," he said, still yelling. As gently as he could, he rolled her onto her back. Immediately he cursed. The shot had been to the chest. "It's okay," he said, surprised when her eyes opened. "You're going to be okay. Matt's called in some help."

Mara smiled up at him, but it was as soft as a whisper. Her eyelids fluttered closed.

Billy couldn't help the fear that tore from his mouth.

"No, stay with me!" Billy pulled her into his lap. Matt appeared at his side and, without words, put pressure on the wound. "Come on, Mara," he said, trying to keep her conscious. Despite Matt's attempt, blood poured out around the detective's hand.

The sight alone tore at Billy worse than any pain he'd ever known.

"You promised you'd never leave me again," he said to her. "You can't leave me again. You promised!"

But Mara kept quiet.

Chapter Twenty-Three

Alexa's hair was a mess. Billy was man enough to admit that that was his fault. He'd finally gotten her used to him brushing out her hair after bath time and right after she woke up, so he'd gotten cocky and tried to do something a bit more adventurous that morning. He'd searched hairstyles for little girls and found a video that showed him how to do a fishtail braid.

Now, looking down at her sleeping against his chest, Billy accepted that the braid looked more like a rat's tail than a fishtail anything. He sighed. Maybe one day he'd get it right. But, for now, no one who'd visited had given him grief about his fathering. That included his mother, surprisingly enough.

He turned to look at the chair next to his. It was empty. She must have stepped out to get coffee or another book while he and Alexa dozed off in his own chair. There was just something about hospital machines and their beeping that created a noise that carried him off to sleep.

Then again, he hadn't gotten much sleep in the last few days.

Billy's eyes traveled to the hospital bed in front of him.

He'd positioned his chair next to Mara's feet so he was facing her. He wanted to know the second she woke up. He wanted to be there for her. If it hadn't been for Alexa, he wouldn't have left her side during the last few days.

Billy closed his eyes again and rested his chin on top of his daughter's head. It was nice to feel her against him after everything that had happened.

Beck's and Marsden's bodies had been collected and buried outside Riker County with their families. Beck turned out to be Kevin Rickman, a college dropout who had tried to desperately follow his father's long criminal career. But, like his father, he'd been killed over power, money and drugs. Beck had only focused on Bryan Copeland's legacy because his father had helped Bryan at the beginning of his drug running, right before he'd been killed. Bryan hadn't ever met Beck, but was able to pick the man's father out of an old picture. Kevin had used an old friend of his father's to get a message to Bryan in prison. Then Bryan had used his connections to relay the stash's location and then call Billy and warn him.

Billy felt the letter folded in his wallet like it was on fire. It was from Bryan to Mara and had been sent to Billy's office. As guilty as he'd felt about reading it, Billy was glad he had. Bryan hadn't given Mara any grief and he hadn't apologized for his past. He'd only said he was glad she was okay and asked if she would send him pictures of both herself and Alexa.

Billy would never like Bryan, but he was glad he'd finally put his daughter's life above his own. So much so that Billy called in a lot of favors, including some of Sheriff Rockwell's, and gotten the news that Bryan Copeland's stash had been found, or even ever existed, kept secret. Just until Bryan could be moved to a prison out of state. Then Billy would personally let everyone know, including anyone with bad intentions, that there was no reason to ever dig on Leigh Cullen's property again. Otherwise there would always be someone who would look for it. The stash had been right where Bryan had told him. A handful of deputies had spent the night digging out a metal container that held more money than Billy would probably make in a lifetime. Plus enough Moxy and other assorted drugs to help any budding drug runner start out strong.

Billy had just started to think about all the paperwork he'd have to fill out when a sound made his eyes flash open.

"Mara," he said, surprised.

Mara, propped up on a pillow, was looking right at him. There was a smile across her lips.

"Don't—" she started but coughed. Billy was already getting up, trying not to jostle Alexa too much. She squirmed once before he laid her down on the love seat on the other side of the room.

"Here," Billy said, voice low, as he grabbed his cup of water and popped a straw into it. He held it up to Mara and she drank a few sips.

"Thanks," she said. "My mouth was really dry."

Billy put the water down on the table and sat on the edge of the bed to face her. He couldn't help but smile. She was the most beautiful woman he'd ever seen.

"I didn't want you to move," Mara said, giving her own smile. "You two were so cute."

Billy glanced back at Alexa and felt a bit sheepish.

"I tried to braid her hair," he explained. "It looked better yesterday."

Mara's brow furrowed. She looked around the room and then down at herself.

"How bad is it?" she whispered.

Billy felt his smile falter.

"You're expected to fully recover. But…" Billy let his hand hover over her chest. The doctor said there'd be a scar there but she'd been damned lucky. The second woman to get the same diagnosis in a week on his watch. "There were a few close calls to get you there."

Billy felt the pain and fear and anguish he'd experienced when Mara had flatlined twice in the ambulance. He'd nearly lost his mind with worry as he'd paced outside surgery afterward.

"I'm okay now, then," Mara said softly. She reached out and patted the top of his hand. Billy realized that, even though she was the one in the hospital bed, she was trying to comfort him.

It made his smile come back and he finally did something he should have done two years before. Reaching into his pocket, he pulled out a small box. He held it up to Mara. Her eyes widened.

"I always thought I'd do something elaborate and romantic when I proposed to you but dammit, Mara,

I can't wait anymore." Billy opened the box. He'd tell her later that he'd bought her the ring two years before, but for now he had to tell her what he wanted in the future. "You don't have to marry me now, tomorrow or even next year, but Mara Copeland, I sure do need you to be my wife." He took the ring out and held it up. "Marry me and let's grow old together?"

Mara's expression softened. Those beautiful lips turned up into the smallest of smiles. When she answered, Billy couldn't help but laugh.

"Sounds good to me, Sheriff."

THE CHRISTMAS TREE was going to fall over. Its branches hung down with the weight of too many ornaments, half from Billy's childhood and the others they'd bought together for Alexa. At the time, Mara had been more than happy to fill their cart with bits and bobbles, but now she was worried the sheer weight of them all was going to kill their tree. Even if it was fake.

"Personally, I think it looks amazing."

Mara turned and smiled. Billy was grinning ear to ear. "I'm sure everyone at the party is going to be jealous that their trees aren't as great as this one." He opened his arms wide, motioning to the tree. Mara caught sight of the wedding band on his finger. It made her glance at hers before answering him. The sight made her feel a warmth spread through her. Every single time.

"That their trees *weren't* as good," she corrected him. "You know, considering it's the end of February and no one has decorations up anymore. Or are celebrating Christmas."

Billy waved his hand dismissively.

"I wasn't about to let my first Christmas with my girls go by without a proper celebration," he said, defiance in his voice. Billy sidled up beside her and placed his arm around her waist. "Plus, I think we deserve a pass to do that, don't you?"

Mara's smile grew.

It had been almost three months since Mara had woken up in the hospital. In that time, several things had happened. The first was that she'd learned Christmas had come and gone while she'd been unconscious. Claire had still taken the day to shower her in gifts and love, but Billy had told everyone that he'd wait until the three of them could celebrate together. As a family.

The idea of their first Christmas together had made her cry, which had, in turn, alarmed the sheriff, but she'd promised they were tears of happiness. Something she realized she'd always feel after Suzy, of all people, had been ordained and married them on the back porch of Billy's house. It had been a short and sweet ceremony. Claire had cried while holding Alexa, while Detective Walker and Captain Jones had been the official witnesses.

Since then, life had moved quickly. Mara quit her job, broke her lease and together with off-duty sheriff's department employees, Billy and she had moved all of her belongings into the Reed family home.

While she felt the love from the department, a part

of Mara had been more than worried that the residents of Carpenter wouldn't ever accept her because of who she was. Especially after the news that she and Billy had a child had traveled through the town like wildfire. However, so far no one had said a rude thing to her. And if they even looked like they were thinking about it, Leigh Cullen would puff up, ready to point out that Mara had died—twice if you counted her heart stopping—to save her son, and if they didn't like her they'd have to deal with Leigh. She'd only used that speech once on a man who hadn't meant any disrespect, but Mara couldn't deny it made her feel good that Leigh didn't seem to hold any more animosity toward her. In fact, while Mara had been in the hospital, Leigh had visited her almost every day.

They'd talked about the serious things first—the sorrys and thank yous for anything and everything that had happened—and then moved on to the personal sides of who they were. It turned out Leigh had been wanting to start her own business—something creative and hands-on—but hadn't found a worthwhile fit. When she found out that Mara had wanted to start up an interior design shop, Leigh had decided that not only could they be friends but they could be business partners, too.

Once Mara was out of the hospital, Leigh proved to have meant every word she'd said. They were already working up the design for an office space downtown. It wasn't large, but it was a start. One Mara was looking forward to. One that her father also praised in a letter. Mara didn't know what their particular future held, especially concerning Alexa, but she couldn't deny she missed her father. They'd agreed to start writing to each other. It, too, was a new start.

Which left one last, life-altering decision that had surprised them. Tough-as-nails, sweet-as-honey Claire Reed. Instead of going back home, she'd pulled a Mara and sold her house, instead.

"I've been bored in retirement anyways," she'd told them one night at supper. "Plus, now that I have a grandbaby, you won't be able to keep me away." She was currently living in the guesthouse but promised she was looking for a place of her own. Though Mara had to admit, it was nice having someone to help with Alexa when she and Billy wanted some alone time.

Which was just as much fun as she'd remembered.

Mara sighed, the warmth of the man next to her seeping into her heart. It made his gaze shift downward.

"Who would have thought that we'd really end up together?" Mara mused.

"I knew we would," he said, matter-of-factly.

"You have to admit, it was quite the journey," she said. "Ups and downs and bad men with guns. Not to mention your mother."

Billy let out a hoot of laughter.

"I hadn't seen *that* one coming," he admitted. "But…"

Mara let out a small yelp of excitement as Billy spun her around. His lips covered hers in a kiss that she'd never forget. When it ended, he stayed close.

"But, as for us, I always knew we'd be here eventually," he whispered, lips pulling up into his famous smirk. It was a sight she was ready to see every day for the rest of her life. "Merry Christmas, Mrs. Reed."

Mara didn't miss a beat.

"Merry Christmas, Sheriff."

* * * * *

Look for THE DEPUTY'S WITNESS,
the next book in Tyler Anne Snell's miniseries
THE PROTECTORS OF RIKER COUNTY,
in December, wherever
Harlequin Intrigue books are sold!

And don't miss the books in her most
recent miniseries, ORION SECURITY:

PRIVATE BODYGUARD
FULL FORCE FATHERHOOD
BE ON THE LOOKOUT: BODYGUARD
SUSPICIOUS ACTIVITIES

Available now from Harlequin Intrigue!

COMING NEXT MONTH FROM

⊞ HARLEQUIN®

INTRIGUE

Available November 21, 2017

#1749 ALWAYS A LAWMAN
Blue River Ranch • by Delores Fossen
Years ago, Jodi Canton and Sheriff Gabriel Beckett were torn apart by a
shocking murder and false conviction. Can they now face the true killer and
rekindle the love they thought they'd lost?

#1750 REDEMPTION AT HAWK'S LANDING
Badge of Justice • by Rita Herron
The murder of her father has brought Honey Granger back to her small
Texas town, but despite his attraction to Honey the hot Sheriff Harrison
Hawk has his own motives for looking into her father's death—the
disappearance of his sister.

#1751 MILITARY GRADE MISTLETOE
The Precinct • by Julie Miller
Master Sergeant Harry Lockheart was the only survivor of the IED that
killed his team—but he credits Daisy Gunderson's kind letters to his actual
recovery. And now that he's finally met the woman of his dreams, he's not
about to let a stalker destroy their dreams for the future.

#1752 PROTECTOR'S INSTINCT
Omega Sector: Under Siege • by Janie Crouch
When former police detective Zane Wales couldn't protect Caroline Gill, he
left both her and the force behind, unable to face his failure. But now that a
psychopath has Caroline in his sights, can Zane find the courage to face the
past and protect the woman he loves still?

#1753 MS. DEMEANOR
Mystery Christmas • by Danica Winters
Rainier Fitzgerald manages to attract both a heap of trouble and the
attention of his parole officer, Laura Blade, only hours after his release. Can
the two of them crack the cold case on Dunrovin ranch or will Christmas be
behind bars?

#1754 THE DEPUTY'S WITNESS
The Protectors of Riker County • by Tyler Anne Snell
Testifying against a trio of lethal bank robbers has drawn a target on
Alyssa Garner's back, and the only man who can save her from the
crosshairs is cop Caleb Foster, who harbors secrets of his own...

Get 2 Free Books,

HARLEQUIN

INTRIGUE

Plus 2 Free Gifts—

just for trying the Reader Service!

H HARLEQUIN®

INTRIGUE

*Years ago, Jodi Canton and Sheriff Gabriel Beckett
were torn apart by a shocking murder and false
conviction. Can they now face the true killer and
rekindle the love they thought they'd lost?*

*Read on for a sneak preview of
ALWAYS A LAWMAN,
the first book in the **BLUE RIVER RANCH** series from
New York Times bestselling author Delores Fossen!*

She had died here. Temporarily, anyway.

But she was alive now, and Jodi Canton could feel the nerves just beneath the surface of her skin. With the Smith & Wesson gripped in her hand, she inched closer to the dump site where he had left her for dead.

There were no signs of the site now. Nearly ten years had passed, and the thick Texas woods had reclaimed the ground. It didn't look nearly so sinister dotted with wildflowers and a honeysuckle vine coiling over it. No drag marks.

No blood.

The years had washed it all away, but Jodi could see it, smell it and even taste it as if it were that sweltering July night when a killer had come within a breath of ending her life.

The nearby house had succumbed to time and the elements, too. It'd been a home then. Now the white paint was blistered, several of the windows on the bottom floor closed off with boards that had grayed with age. Of course, she hadn't expected this place to ever feel like anything but the crime scene that it had once been.

Considering that two people had been murdered inside.

Jodi adjusted the grip on the gun when she heard the footsteps. They weren't hurried, but her visitor wasn't trying to sneak up on her, either. Jodi had been listening for that. Listening for everything that could get her killed.

Permanently this time.

Just in case she was wrong about who this might be, Jodi pivoted and took aim at him.

"You shouldn't have come here," he said. His voice was husky and deep, part lawman's growl, part Texas drawl.

The man was exactly who she thought it might be. Sheriff Gabriel Beckett. No surprise that he had arrived, since this was Beckett land, and she'd parked in plain sight on the side of the road that led to the house. Even though the Becketts no longer lived here, Gabriel would have likely used the road to get to his current house.

"You came," Jodi answered, and she lowered her gun.

Muttering some profanity with that husky drawl, Gabriel walked to her side, his attention on the same area where hers was fixed. Or at least it was until he looked at her the same exact moment that she looked at him.

Their gazes connected.

And now it was Jodi who wanted to curse. Really? After all this time that punch of attraction was still there? She had huge reasons for the attraction to go away and not a single reason for it to stay.

Yet it remained.

Don't miss
ALWAYS A LAWMAN,
available December 2017 wherever
Harlequin® Intrigue books and ebooks are sold.

www.Harlequin.com

HIEXP1117

LOVE
Harlequin
romance?

Join our Harlequin community to share your thoughts and connect with other romance readers!

Be the first to find out about promotions, news, and exclusive content!

Sign up for the Harlequin e-newsletter and download a free book from any series at

www.TryHarlequin.com

THE WORLD IS BETTER
WITH
Romance

Harlequin has everything from contemporary, passionate and heartwarming to suspenseful and inspirational stories.

Whatever your mood,
we have a romance just for you!

Connect with us to find your next great read,
special offers and more.

f /HarlequinBooks

🐦 @HarlequinBooks

www.HarlequinBlog.com

www.Harlequin.com/Newsletters

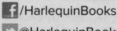
⬦ HARLEQUIN

A *Romance* FOR EVERY MOOD™

www.Harlequin.com